LOST AT SEA

A huge swell hit Jessica and Winston's lifeboat. Winston's knees buckled, and he lost his balance. Jessica tried her hardest to steady the boat, but it was no use. As Winston fell heavily to one side, it capsized!

The last thing Jessica saw before she hit the icy water was the look of terror in Elizabeth's eyes.

She tried to hang on to the overturned lifeboat, but her hands slipped off the slick rubber. Jessica felt as helpless as a rag doll when a churning wave hit her full force and carried her away from the lifeboat.

The wave passed over her, and she treaded water for a minute, gasping for breath. Her eyes stinging from the salt and the driving rain, she peered around her through the fog. She couldn't see far, but all she could see was ocean. Winston, the lifeboat, and the rest of her class were gone.

Bantam Books in the Sweet Valley High Series
Ask your bookseller for the books you have missed

SWEET VALLEY HIGH

LOST AT SEA

Written by
Kate William

Created by
FRANCINE PASCAL

BANTAM BOOKS
NEW YORK • TORONTO • LONDON • SYDNEY • AUCKLAND

RL 6, IL age 12 and up

LOST AT SEA
A Bantam Book / June 1989

Sweet Valley High is a registered trademark of Francine Pascal

Conceived by Francine Pascal

Produced by Daniel Weiss Associates, Inc.,
27 West 20th Street, New York, NY 10011

Cover art by James Mathewuse

ISBN 0-553-27970-X

Published simultaneously in the United States and Canada

Bantam Books are published by Bantam Books, a division of Bantam Doubleday Dell Publishing Group, Inc. Its trademark, consisting of the words "Bantam Books" and the portrayal of a rooster, is Registered in U.S. Patent and Trademark Office and in other countries. Marca Registrada. Bantam Books, 666 Fifth Avenue, New York, New York 10103.

PRINTED IN THE UNITED STATES OF AMERICA

O   0 9 8 7 6 5 4 3 2 1

LOST AT SEA

One

"Jessica, you're going on a science-class field trip, not entering the Miss Teenage America contest!" Elizabeth Wakefield reminded her twin sister with a slightly exasperated smile.

Jessica had been poised in front of the mirror for twenty minutes in the bathroom the sixteen-year-old twins shared. She gave her long lashes one final dab with the mascara brush, then turned to Elizabeth.

"Liz, for somebody who wants to be a famous writer, sometimes you have absolutely no imagination! This may just be a class field trip to *you*, but *I* can see its deeper potential," Jessica declared in a sophisticated tone. "For ex-

1

ample, it's a chance to work on my tan, *and* a chance to work on Ken Matthews!" Wiggling her eyebrows suggestively, Jessica strolled past Elizabeth out of the bathroom.

"Ken Matthews?" Elizabeth repeated, surprised. A classmate of theirs at Sweet Valley High, Ken was captain and star quarterback of the school football team. Jessica had dated Ken occasionally in the past, but Elizabeth had thought that was it as far as their "romance" was concerned. "Since when are you interested in Ken again?" she asked.

"Since I checked out the list of people signed up for the field trip and he was the cutest one on it," Jessica answered matter-of-factly from her bedroom.

Elizabeth laughed as she pulled her shoulder-length blond hair up into a ponytail. Trust Jessica to have anything but academics in mind! Elizabeth wasn't exactly surprised, though. Their attitude toward school was only one way in which she and her twin differed.

It was true that, on the outside, the beautiful Sweet Valley High juniors were nearly mirror images of one another. Both were five and a half feet tall with perfect, willowy size-six figures. Both had silky sun-streaked blond hair and eyes the same blue-green shade as the nearby Pacific Ocean. But when it came to the inside, they were definitely individuals, as different as avocados and oranges. Elizabeth, the elder twin by four minutes, was generous, thoughtful, and responsible. She was serious about her schoolwork *and* about her steady boyfriend, Jeffrey French. While she enjoyed a good party as much as anyone, she was just as happy to take long walks with Jeffrey or spend an evening listening to music and talking to her best friend, Enid Rollins. Elizabeth dreamed of someday being a professional journalist, and with that goal in mind she spent a good deal of her spare time writing for *The Oracle*, Sweet Valley High's newspaper.

Jessica, on the other hand, wasn't interested in the future. She lived for the moment. Being spontaneous sometimes got her into trouble, but she could always—well, *almost* always—count on Elizabeth to help her out. While Elizabeth composed "Eyes and Ears," her weekly gossip column for *The Oracle*, Jessica devoted her extracurricular energies to the cheerleading squad, of which she was co-captain.

As for boys, Jessica had been famous for playing the field until she had met A. J. Morgan. For a while she and A. J. had been a steady couple. But even though she had cared more deeply for A. J. than she ever had for another boy, Jessica still had been tempted to wander. She had learned her lesson the hard way after a brief, thoughtless fling with a handsome surfer became complicated, finally endangering both her life and Elizabeth's. Now, although Jessica's heart still ached a little when she thought about A. J., she knew breaking up with him had been for the best. She wasn't grown up enough to commit herself to a relationship with just one person. It was more fun to be free and to flirt whenever she felt like it.

Toward that end, Jessica had been pleased to hear that Ken Matthews would also be going on the marine biology field trip that afternoon. Tall, blond, and well built, Ken was far and away the most interesting and attractive boy in the small group of students signed up for the trip. It was part of Jessica's creed to make the best of any situation, and she intended to do just that. She would have done almost anything to get out of the Sunday afternoon field trip to Anacapa Island, but unfortunately, her midterm chemistry grade was far from respectable. Her teacher, Bob Russo, had practically ordered her to sign up for the optional trip. "You need all the extra credit you can get, Jessica," he had pointed out dryly.

4

Jessica reluctantly admitted to herself that she was lucky. Mr. Russo was willing to give her extra credit since the field trip had nothing to do with chemistry. He could have made her spend hours in the lab, doing extra experiments!

Elizabeth, on the other hand, had an A average in chemistry. She had signed up for the trip because visiting the small, deserted island sounded like fun. Studying the tide pools and ecology of the unspoiled island might give her an idea for an article. And, of course, the fact that Enid was going didn't hurt, either.

Elizabeth grabbed a notebook from her work table and went downstairs. She glanced at the clock in the kitchen. It was twelve-forty-five, and they were due at the marina at one o'clock sharp. "Jess, we're going to miss the boat, *literally!*" she shouted up the staircase to her sister, who was still dawdling in her bedroom.

A few moments later Jessica appeared and began a leisurely descent of the stairs. She didn't own a wristwatch, for she didn't share her twin's respect for punctuality. As far as Jessica was concerned, she was never late, because nothing ever started until she got there. "Hold your horses, Lizzie!" she said cheerfully. "Mr. Russo won't leave without us. He'd just have to arrange another field trip so I could get enough extra credit to pass chemistry!"

Elizabeth shook her head with good-natured disapproval, as much at Jessica's appearance as at her words. "Now, that's a practical field trip outfit," Elizabeth observed.

Jessica glanced down at herself. She was wearing new flimsy thong sandals the same cherry red as her toenail polish. Her very short, very snug iced-denim shorts made the most of her slim, bronzed legs. On top, a skimpy bandeau left her shoulders bare for optimal tanning exposure—and optimal exposure for admiring male eyes. In contrast, Elizabeth, always a conservative dresser, wore a shell-pink scooped-neck top, Bermuda shorts, and sneakers.

"Don't worry," Jessica assured Elizabeth. She waved the gauzy white shirt she was holding in her right hand along with her sunglasses and a bottle of tanning oil. "I won't scandalize Mr. Russo by showing up half naked for his field trip." She smiled slyly. "I'll cover up until he's not looking!"

Elizabeth grinned and then grabbed Jessica's arm, pulling her toward the door. "At this point I don't care if you go in your underwear. Let's just get moving!"

They detoured through the backyard to say

goodbye to their mother and father, who were lingering over coffee and the Sunday paper by the pool. Then the twins hopped into the old red Fiat convertible they shared, which was parked in the driveway alongside their split-level home. Elizabeth took the wheel, which was fine with Jessica. She leaned back in her seat as Elizabeth cautiously backed into the street. Tipping her head back and closing her eyes, Jessica enjoyed the feel of the sun on her face and the wind in her hair. It was another beautiful day in Sweet Valley, California. She might have preferred to be at the beach all day, but as long as she was outside getting some sun, even a school trip was all right.

And who knows, Jessica thought, opening her eyes just as the Fiat topped a hill, affording her a glimpse of the Pacific Ocean, sparkling blue beyond the lush green valley. She pictured herself with Ken, strolling hand in hand down a postcard-perfect island beach. *This field trip could turn out to be a real adventure!*

"Everybody's here, *finally*," Bob Russo announced crisply, glancing at Jessica and Elizabeth. "Now, let's see. We've got sixteen juniors

7

from three different science sections, just right for breaking up into four teams of four."

As Mr. Russo checked their names off on the list on his clipboard, Elizabeth walked over to greet Enid, while Jessica joined her friend Lila Fowler. Lila was standing at the end of the dock, looking bored. She greeted Jessica with a yawn, covering her mouth with one elegantly manicured hand. "This is going to be the worst," Lila moaned. "A whole day wasted just to raise my science grade a measly point or two. I can't believe Amy wormed her way out of this," she said, referring to their friend Amy Sutton. Amy had told Mr. Russo that due to a family obligation, she would be unable to make the trip. But both Lila and Jessica knew she was spending the day at the beach with Bruce Patman.

"Oh, come on, Lila." Jessica waved an arm at the wind-ruffled water. "Look at it this way: Amy will have to write a five-page paper to get her extra credit, and we just have to go cruising around in a boat for ours."

"Yes, but look at the *boat*." The breeze blew a long strand of Lila's wavy light brown hair across her face as she nodded disdainfully toward the end of the pier. "We're going to be crammed in like sardines!"

The chartered powerboat looked roomy enough

to Jessica, but she could see how it might not meet Lila's standards. To Lila, the daughter of one of the wealthiest men in Southern California, a boat ride was usually a Caribbean cruise on an ocean liner. Lila had everything money could buy, and she was lavished with gifts and spending money by her father. Jessica alternated between envying Lila's status and possessions and being irritated by her snobby act.

Now Jessica shrugged off Lila's whining. She scanned the rest of the group through the dark lenses of her sunglasses. Elizabeth and Enid were chatting with Tom McKay, a good-looking tennis player whom Jessica had casually dated. A half dozen other kids she didn't know very well were milling about. On the far side of the pier Ken Matthews and Aaron Dallas were laughing at something Winston Egbert had just told them.

Jessica tapped Lila on the shoulder. "There's my reason for taking a positive attitude toward this otherwise boring-beyond-belief trip." She pointed discreetly in Ken's direction.

Lila followed Jessica's finger. "Who, Winston Egbert?" she teased.

Jessica snorted. "That buffoon? Ha-ha. Guess again."

"Ken Matthews?" When Jessica nodded, Lila

yawned again. "Oh, Jess, he's such old news. Can't you do any better than that?"

Jessica took another look. " 'Fraid not," she said. "Aaron Dallas and Tom McKay are taken, and Mr. Russo's too old."

Lila giggled. "Nope," Jessica concluded, "I assure you I've given this some thought. It's Ken or no one."

Lila raised a slender eyebrow. "You're sure not wasting any time hunting down another boyfriend."

Lila's insinuating tone infuriated Jessica. She distinctly recalled several times when Lila had started seeing someone new only seconds after breaking up with a previous boyfriend. "Don't preach to me," Jessica warned her. "A. J. and I are completely over, ancient history. It's been ages!"

Lila laughed airily at Jessica's exaggeration. "I was just kidding you. Go for it. Good luck."

Just then Jessica tuned back in to Mr. Russo. "So, for the teams," he was saying. Her ears perked up. Obviously there wasn't a moment to lose if she wanted to be assigned to the same team as Ken. She could just join Ken, Aaron, and Winston—that was four people right there. She liked Aaron, and she would even put up with Winston's looniness to be with Ken.

"You said go for it, Lila. Watch this!"

Pushing her sunglasses up on her head, Jessica strolled across the pier toward the three boys. It appeared that Winston, known as the class clown, was in the middle of another joke. He was waving his long skinny arms and making goofy faces while Ken and Aaron guffawed. "Hi, guys!" Jessica said brightly, flashing Ken her most brilliant smile. "Am I in time for the punchline?"

Before Winston had a chance to finish his story, Mr. Russo resumed speaking. "Team one"—Mr. Russo scanned the group in a businesslike way—"Enid Rollins, Elizabeth Wakefield, Ken Matthews, and Aaron Dallas. Team two: Jessica Wakefield, Winston Egbert, Lois Waller, Randy Mason. Team three . . ."

Jessica's mouth dropped open. Winston Egbert and *who*? Mr. Russo had to be kidding. There she was, practically standing on Ken Matthews's gorgeous toes, and Mr. Russo had gone and stuck her on a team with two nobodies and the class clown! Shy, chubby Lois Waller, the daughter of the high-school dietician, had about as much personality as a marshmallow. And all Jessica knew about nerdy Randy Mason was that he was active in the Sweet Valley High computer club. This was pathetic, she thought. Was there no justice in the world?

"So, finish your joke, Egbert," Aaron urged him.

Inwardly fuming, Jessica turned away, not bothering to listen. It was only too obvious: The joke was on her.

By the time the charter boat, the *Maverick*, chugged away from the dock ten minutes later, Jessica had regained her good spirits. Maybe she and Ken wouldn't be studying the same tide pool, but they would still have plenty of time to talk on the boat, since the ride was an hour each way.

In a lecturelike tone, Mr. Russo went over the buddy system and on-board safety procedures, pointing out where the life jackets and self-inflating lifeboats were stored. Then his face relaxed into an unusually jovial smile. "Class dismissed," he said, adding, "but only until we get to Anacapa Island."

When Mr. Russo turned his back to talk to the *Maverick*'s captain, Jessica whipped off her gauze shirt. "Time for some sun and fun," she announced to Lila, Elizabeth, and Enid, with whom she was sitting on one side of the boat. Out of the corner of her eye she could see Ken and Aaron lounging near the bow. "Feel like taking a little walk, Lila?"

Lila nodded, but before they could take a step, Winston bounded into their path. "Hey, buddy!" He threw his arm around Jessica's shoulders. "You weren't thinking of going anywhere without me, were you?"

Jessica shrugged Winston's arm off with a scowl. When Mr. Russo had split the team into pairs for the buddy system, she had ended up with Winston as her buddy. She didn't mind him in small doses; he could be pretty funny sometimes. Unfortunately, the field trip had only just started, and already Jessica felt as if she'd had enough of him. "Winston, we only have to be buddies in case of an emergency," she said, stepping around him.

"A buddy's a buddy," Winston insisted. "I feel it's my duty not to let you out of my sight. What if you fell overboard because your buddy wasn't looking out for you?"

Jessica rolled her eyes at Lila. "Thanks, but I'll take my chances," she told him. Grabbing Lila's arm, she practically ran across the boat toward Ken and Aaron, figuring Winston would get the message.

But no sooner had Jessica greeted Ken, giving him her second dazzling smile of the day, than

Winston poked his head between them. With his San Diego Padres baseball cap turned backward on his head, he looked even more ridiculous than usual.

"Jessica Wakefield," Winston began, imitating Mr. Russo's deep, authoritative voice, "I'm going to have to assign you a week of detention for violating the rules of the buddy system."

"So, Ken, don't tell me you're bombing in chemistry, too," Jessica said, turning her back on Winston.

Ken, who had been leaning on the rail of the boat, turned to face Jessica. "You got it," he confirmed with a wry grin. "You didn't think I came on this field trip for the joy of learning?"

Jessica laughed. "I know you better than that, Matthews," she assured him with a meaningful flutter of her eyelashes.

"Hey, buddy, enough chitchat."

Jessica whirled around, annoyed. Winston, his arms piled high with bright orange life jackets, was standing right behind her. Before she could protest, he slipped two life preservers around her neck. "Safety first, Jessica," Winston reminded her.

Ken, Lila, and Aaron doubled over with laughter. Jessica, however, was not amused. "Egbert, you *idiot!*" she exclaimed, waving her arms to

14

ward off a third life jacket. "Why don't you go jump in the ocean?"

In a flash Winston was at the railing, his hands clasped in front of him and his knees bent as if ready to jump. Jessica groaned as she wriggled out of the life jackets. It was all she could do to restrain herself from reaching forward to give Winston a push!

In the meantime Ken and Aaron had launched into a discussion with Lila. Jessica casually walked over to them and interrupted the conversation. "Anyone want to go with me to ask the captain if we can drive the boat for a while?" she asked, looking right at Ken.

"I do, I do!" Winston answered, running over. Before Jessica could say she had changed her mind, Winston was steering her toward the upper deck. "C'mon, buddy!"

"I have a feeling this is going to be a long afternoon," Jessica muttered to herself.

Two

"Land, ho!" Winston shouted, standing at the bow of the *Maverick* with one hand shielding his eyes from the sun.

Jessica could hardly wait to get to shore. As soon as Mr. Russo helped each team locate a tide pool, they would be on their own. She figured she could take a quick look at her tide pool and then ditch Winston, Lois, and Randy—and the sooner the better. She could copy their notes later on that afternoon. She planned on sneaking off to sunbathe.

As the boat pulled into a cove on the south end of Anacapa Island, Jessica gasped. The small, unpopulated island looked like a tropical paradise! A half-moon of sugar-white sand was edged with palm trees and a jungle of exotic plants and flowers. On one side of the beach was a rocky point. Mr. Russo pointed to it. "A perfect spot for tide pools!" he commented eagerly.

Captain Marsden cut the engine, and everybody jumped off the boat and waded to shore. Jessica stayed as close as possible to Ken, but Winston stayed just as close to her. Jessica didn't mind, though. In a few minutes she would get rid of Winston and the rest of her classmates—except Ken. It wouldn't be hard to lure him away from his team. They could go for a romantic walk in the woods. *Who knows what will happen?* Jessica thought.

Mr. Russo clapped his hands to get everyone's attention. "OK, kids, because this is an extra-credit field trip and not a formal lab, I'm not going to require a write-up from each of you." Jessica smiled. Mr. Russo was practically giving her permission to spend the afternoon having fun.

"Instead," Mr. Russo continued, "one person from each team will act as scribe, recording the team's data. Two hours from now we'll meet back here for a wrap-up session. While the entire team will collaborate on the research, the scribe for each team will present the team's findings at the wrap-up. I'm assigning the scribes at random. Let's see." He paused for only a moment before decisively announcing, "Ken for team one, Jessica for team two, Tom for team three, and Katrina for team four. Good luck!"

Jessica swallowed a scream. Now she would be shackled to Winston, Randy, and Lois for the entire field trip. Not only that, but she would actually have to *work!*

After casting a withering look at Mr. Russo, Jessica trudged down the sand toward the rocks. Winston carried the team's equipment: a portable microscope, a box of plastic slides, a plastic ruler, and a pocket-sized textbook to help them identify various plants and shore organisms. They found a tide pool quickly, and Mr. Russo approved it.

"Here you go, scribe." With a flourish, Winston offered Jessica a pad of paper and a sharp pencil. "It's all yours!"

Jessica snatched the paper and the pencil from him. "Well, let's get this over with!" she said irritably.

"First we have to describe the tide pool's appearance," said Lois, peering meekly at Jessica through her oversize glasses and shaggy brown hair.

"Fine. So describe." Jessica gripped the pencil, ready to write.

"A tide pool is a microcosm of ocean ecology," Winston said in a corny French accent, imitating Jacques Cousteau. "In a tide pool seaweed, shellfish, and microscopic organisms live in harmony. As the tide recedes and the sun warms the pool—"

"Shut up and describe the stupid pool!" Jessica demanded.

"Well, it's round," Winston said with a deadpan expression.

Jessica recorded the information and then waited for Winston to continue.

"And it's wet," he added, smiling mischievously.

"Winston!" Jessica warned.

Randy held out a plastic ruler. "The pool is six inches deep at the deepest end and two inches deep at the shallow end," he said helpfully. "And it has a sandy bottom."

"So much for its appearance." Jessica decided that if she had to be team scribe, at least she could use her position to hurry things along. "Now, what's in it?"

All four leaned over the pool to observe. For a moment even Jessica was captivated by its peaceful perfection. Feathery plants swayed gently back and forth, tiny crabs shuffled sideways among the shells and snails, and a school of tiny minnows darted erratically around the pool. Suddenly there was a loud splash, and saltwater flew into Jessica's face. When she opened her eyes again, she saw that the crystal-clear pool had turned into a muddy, murky puddle.

Jessica stared disbelievingly. But it was true. One of Winston's feet, basketball sneaker and all, was planted smack in the middle of the tide pool.

"Winston!" Jessica, Lois, and Randy exclaimed in unison.

Looking sheepish, Winston gingerly removed his foot. "Gee, I didn't mean to do that. I was bending forward for a closer look, and I lost my balance." He laughed. "Next thing I knew, I was taking a swim!"

"It's not funny, Egbert," Jessica snapped, throwing down her paper and pencil. "You ruined our project! You've probably killed all our crabs and snails. *And* you got me soaking wet!"

Angrily she brushed the salty droplets off her

20

bare arms, ignoring Winston's apologies. "If we don't get our extra credit, it'll be all your fault," Jessica accused him.

Randy finished wiping his glasses off with his T-shirt and slipped them back on. He looked shyly at Jessica. "I bet if we let the tide pool alone for fifteen minutes or so, the sand will settle, and we'll be able to study it again. Why don't we take a short break?" he suggested.

"That's a very good idea," Jessica agreed. She flashed Winston her strongest if-looks-could-kill glare. "And, Winston, I'm warning you. No, I'm threatening you! One more move like that and I'm never speaking to you again. I just don't know what Maria sees in you!"

Jessica stomped off as dramatically as she could, considering that her flimsy sandals kept slipping on the rocks and she had to wave her arms to keep her balance. She had wondered more than once before what pretty, dark-haired Maria Santelli, a fellow cheerleader, saw in her boyfriend, Winston. It certainly wasn't his looks. Winston was lanky and awkward with no muscles worth mentioning. And it couldn't be his manners; he wasn't exactly suave. *I guess he makes her laugh*, Jessica thought. Winston was definitely a comedian. He delivered one-liners the way a major-league pitcher delivered fastballs. He was an institution at Sweet Valley High, invited to every party because he provided free entertainment. *But, boy, I'd rather date a guy with absolutely no sense of humor than one with too much!* Jessica thought. She wished Maria had come on the field trip so Winston would hang all over her instead.

As she put as much space as possible between herself and Winston, Jessica looked for a spot to lie down so she could improve her tan. *It sure would be nice to have some company*, she thought wistfully. It was too bad Ken was busy being his team's scribe. Then Jessica thought of Lila. She was probably dying for an excuse to get out of working, too.

Jessica spotted Lila's team fifty yards away on the other side of the point. Clambering carefully over the rocks, she whispered loudly, "Hey, Lila! Want to join me? I'm going to catch some rays."

Lila sighed. "I wish I could," she said in a soft voice. "But Mr. Science over there"—Lila nodded her head in Tom McKay's direction—"is our scribe, and he's taking this whole thing really seriously. He'd probably snitch to Mr. Russo if I left."

"Sorry," Jessica said, patting Lila on the shoulder. "I'll see you later."

Lila sighed again. "Yeah. So long."

Jessica picked a spot on the beach out of sight of Mr. Russo and laid down on the sand, using her rolled-up gauze shirt as a pillow. The sand felt warm under her back. In a few seconds she relaxed into the sunbathing mode . . . her mind emptying out as she surrendered to the pleasure of the sun and the cool, fresh breeze. If only she didn't have to go back to her tide pool . . .

Something cold and wet and disgusting suddenly landed on Jessica's face. "Eeek!" she cried, sitting up abruptly.

"Hey, buddy, look what I found!" Winston proudly displayed a slimy branch of gelatinous, neon-green seaweed. "Pretty fancy, huh? This isn't your garden-variety seaweed, either. I looked it up in the book."

"Great, Winston." Jessica flopped backward on the sand and closed her eyes.

Winston didn't seem to get the message that Jessica wanted to be left alone. Instead, he sat down next to her. "This is the life," he said, pounding a fist on his chest as if he were Tarzan. "Sailing the seven seas to explore uncharted islands—"

Jessica suddenly sat up at the sound of Elizabeth's voice. Turning her back on Winston, she looked for her twin's group. Finally she was in luck! Elizabeth, Enid, Ken, and Aaron were studying a tide pool not far away. "I just thought of something really urgent I have to ask my sister," Jessica announced, jumping to her feet. "See you back at the tide pool, Winston."

Jessica ran her fingers through her hair, fluffing it up around her face. She brushed a few grains of sand off her legs and quickly adjusted her bandeau.

"Hi, guys, how's it going?" she called out cheerfully as she approached.

Ken looked up and met Jessica's eyes. His smile was warm and friendly. Jessica stopped a few feet away so that Ken could get an optimal view of her body posed against the seductive backdrop of the sea, sand, and palm trees.

"Hi, Jess," Elizabeth said, glancing up from the pool. Her face broke into a smile. Jessica smiled back. Then Jessica noticed that instead of fading, Elizabeth's smile grew wider. Ken, Aaron, and Enid were also grinning.

"What's so funny?" Jessica asked, slightly peeved. Ken was supposed to get stars in his eyes at the sight of her, not start cracking up.

24

At that moment Jessica felt something moving on top of her head. Shrieking, she brushed wildly at her hair with both hands. A big hermit crab flew off her head and landed, wiggling, on the sand.

Jessica spun around. Just as she suspected, Winston had tiptoed up behind her with the crab. Now he was rolling on the sand, helpless with laughter at the outraged expression on Jessica's face.

Everyone else seemed to think it was hilarious, too. Enid and Elizabeth were holding on to each other, laughing.

"Egbert, you're too much," Ken said with a chuckle.

Jessica tried to smile, but it was impossible. How could she hope to impress Ken with shellfish in her hair? Thanks to Winston, she was coming across like the class clown herself!

Jessica's team finally managed to put together a report on their tide pool, despite all of Winston's clumsy mistakes. The second part of the afternoon's assignment required them to pace off a ten-square-yard area in the undergrowth beyond the beach and then write down the names of twenty different plants and insects they could find within it.

Lois looked at her watch. "We only have ten minutes," she observed, sounding doubtful. "Then we have to be back for the wrap-up."

"No problem." Jessica wasn't daunted. "We can do it in five!"

With Jessica leading the way, the group charged into the woods above the beach and quickly marked out a square. Winston, Lois, and Randy shouted out the names of plants and insects while Jessica rapidly took notes. However, after locating fifteen different plants and insect species, they came to a halt.

"C'mon!" Jessica urged the others, cheerleader-style. "We're almost there. Our extra credit is hanging on this. Just five more stupid plant or insect names."

Randy and Lois dutifully dug down again among the ferns and saplings, but Winston had disappeared. *Where is that good-for-nothing?* Jessica wondered, annoyed.

Suddenly there was a loud crash in the trees behind her. It sounded like an animal moving in the underbrush. Jessica pictured a hungry panther coming to get her, or a boa constrictor wriggling closer and closer to her feet. . . . Giving a terrified yelp, she jumped back and headed for the nearest palm tree to take shelter.

"Jessica, what's the matter?"

Tipping her neck back, she looked up and saw Winston, who had shimmied halfway up a tall palm, about to throw another large nut into the bushes. "Scared you, huh, buddy?" he asked gleefully.

"That's it!" Jessica fumed. "Forget finding the last five names. Team two is now formally dissolved! And, Winston, if you know what's good for you, you'll stay up in that tree!"

The other teams were already assembled on the beach when Jessica, Lois, and Randy arrived, with Winston not far behind. As she joined her sister, Jessica noticed for the first time that the breeze, now quickened into a sharp wind coming out of the north, had pushed a low bank of clouds in front of the sun. The drop in temperature was just what she needed to regain her cool after getting steamed up by Winston. She slipped her arms back into the sleeves of her shirt.

Off to one side, Mr. Russo seemed to be conferring with Captain Marsden. Looking at the dark clouds on the horizon, the captain shook his head.

Bob Russo turned to the students. "It looks

like we might be in for a little surprise storm, so we're going to have to cut the field trip short," he announced. "Captain Marsden wants to beat the rain home. We'll postpone the wrap-up until we're back on shore."

Elizabeth seemed disappointed, but Jessica was thrilled. From her point of view, the field trip couldn't be over too soon.

Three

The Pacific Ocean looked completely different on the return trip. Instead of brilliant blue, it was slate gray and extremely choppy. The *Maverick* bounced across the waves, with every bounce sending up huge jets of salt spray.

Jessica was enjoying the wild ride. The wind and the surf—and the fact that Winston was at the other end of the boat—combined to clear her mind of the annoyance she had felt earlier.

"Isn't this fun?" Jessica asked Ken. The wind practically grabbed the words right out of her mouth.

"What?" Even though Ken was sitting right next to her in the boat's stern, he had to lean closer to hear her. Jessica didn't mind.

29

"This is fun," she repeated, putting her lips as near to Ken's ear as she could without actually touching it.

Ken nodded. "There's nothing like being near the water, or on the water, when a storm comes up. It's a pretty cool sight."

Cool was the right word, Jessica thought. The wind had a sharp edge to it, and her gauze top didn't provide much protection. It was a good excuse to snuggle up to Ken, who had one arm stretched casually along the back of the boat behind her neck.

It was the moment she had been waiting for all day, and Jessica was unselfish enough to acknowledge silently that she had Elizabeth to thank. Her twin had cornered Winston at the bow of the boat and was engaging him in conversation. Elizabeth glanced Jessica's way and winked. Jessica smiled gratefully.

She turned to Ken. His blue-gray eyes were narrowed against the wind, which whipped his shaggy blond hair back from his face. He looked even better than usual.

"Ken, I haven't gotten to talk to you much lately," Jessica observed, trying to indicate by her silky tone of voice that she would like to remedy the situation.

"Must be because I've been busy failing science," Ken joked.

"Me, too," Jessica commiserated. "I guess Mr. Russo didn't think it was enough punishment to have to go on this field trip in the first place. He made us both scribes for our teams! I don't know about you, but I'd been planning to get in as little work—and as much play—as possible today."

Ken laughed. "Me, too."

The boat took an extra-hard bounce across a large wave, and Jessica found herself thrown against Ken. He put an arm around her to steady her and then left it there. Ken's body next to hers made Jessica's toes tingle with excitement. She was plenty warm now.

Ken seemed to be feeling the same electricity. "It's been a while, Jess," he began thoughtfully, looking down into her expectant eyes, "since we—you and I—did anything together, just the two of us. Remember the Homecoming dance sophomore year?"

"Do I ever." Jessica giggled. "You ran out of gas driving me home, and I thought you planned it so you could be alone with me!"

Ken grinned. "Until I left you in the car while I walked to the nearest gas station by myself, that is!"

"Right." Jessica knew that getting Ken to stroll down memory lane was the right idea. "And remember," she said with a meaningful smile, "that night at the Beach Disco last spring?"

At a big party at the oceanfront dance club, Ken and Jessica had danced up a storm together. They had ended one slow number out on the deck under the stars. Caught up in the moment, they had shared a long, warm kiss.

Ken did remember, Jessica saw that. The look in his eyes was warm enough to start a forest fire. "Hey, Jess," he said in a husky voice, "Bruce might be putting together a party on Friday night. Would you want to—"

Ken was cut off in midsentence as the *Maverick* hit another giant swell. This time the wave caught the small boat broadside. There were shouts as water washed clear across the deck, soaking everyone on board.

The fire that Ken and Jessica had been starting was put out with a sizzle. Jessica was cold, really cold, right down to her bones. Her teeth chattering, she looked around her. The waves were twice as high as they had been when they left Anacapa Island just a quarter of an hour earlier, and a thick fog had materialized. All of a sudden the rising storm wasn't fun anymore. It was downright scary.

Captain Marsden was on his ship-to-shore radio, shouting to make himself heard over the roar of the wind. "I think we might be in trouble. I'm going to keep the line open. Be ready for an S.O.S.!"

Just then an enormous swell washed over the boat, nearly capsizing it. Jessica screamed and threw her arms around Ken's neck. Ken gripped the railing tightly with both hands to keep from being swept overboard.

The boat was filling rapidly with water. The engine had stalled, and Jessica could see Captain Marsden pulling uselessly on one of the levers on the dashboard. A moment later he turned around. "We're going to have to evacuate!" he shouted, raising his voice above the howl of the wind. There were gasps of fear, and Lila screeched.

Captain Marsden lifted a hand. "Stay calm. I'm radioing for help, and we'll be picked up by the Coast Guard in no time. Just buckle your life jackets tightly and do your best to stay in sight of the *Maverick*. She may stay afloat, but I can't be sure."

There was a mad rush for the life jackets. Mr. Russo started hauling rubber lifeboats and plastic oars out of the charter boat's storage bin.

Ken helped Jessica slip her arms into a canary-yellow life preserver and then put his arms around her in a protective hug. They stood up to their knees in cold water, barely able to keep their balance on the sinking boat. "Don't worry, Jess," Ken said. "We'll be fine."

Jessica was more excited than anxious. Captain Marsden had said the Coast Guard was coming, so there really wasn't any danger involved, she thought. But talk about romantic! She and Ken Matthews, soaking wet and clinging to each other in a tiny lifeboat in the middle of a raging sea. . . .

Mr. Russo had pulled the tab on the first lifeboat, and it inflated rapidly. "OK," he yelled. "Two people and two oars to a lifeboat!"

Jessica and Ken pressed forward along with the others. Then Mr. Russo added, "Buddy system!"

Buddy system. Jessica groaned. Ken gave her a last squeeze and then dashed over to join Enid—leaving Jessica with Winston!

Four lifeboats and eight students had already gone over the side of the *Maverick* when Winston grabbed Jessica's hand. "Here I am, buddy," he said in a tone that was half jovial and half scared. "Never fear, I'll save you!"

"That's what I'm afraid of," Jessica grumbled. But there was no time to bicker. Mr. Russo had the second-to-last lifeboat inflated. He and Captain Marsden would take the last one. Jessica and Winston climbed over the side of the *Maverick* and jumped into the lifeboat.

Winston had a precarious hold on the oars he had grabbed from the science teacher. As he settled himself in, he nearly knocked Jessica out of the lifeboat by jabbing her with an oar.

"Watch what you're doing!" Jessica yelled at him. The wind whipped a strand of wet, salty hair into her mouth. She spit it out, adding, "I swear, Winston, you're more of a health hazard than a tidal wave!"

The storm was growing more violent by the minute. There were towering waves as far as the eye could see. Jessica and Winston's lifeboat bobbed wildly on the water, one minute rising way up and the next sinking so low that they temporarily lost sight of the *Maverick* and the other lifeboats.

As her lifeboat rode to the crest of a swell, Jessica saw Elizabeth waving at her through the fog. Jessica waved back, glad that her sister was secure in a boat with Aaron. The other boat dipped out of sight and then reappeared again a moment later. Elizabeth, her face anxious, was still waving furiously. Now Aaron flailed his arms, too.

"We only have one oar!" Aaron hollered. "Does anyone have an extra?"

Jessica gripped the sides of the lifeboat, her heart in her throat. What if Elizabeth and Aaron were swept away, unable to maneuver their boat with just one oar?

Then Winston let out a triumphant shout. "We've got one!" He waved the oar over his head. "I took three by mistake!"

Jessica was so thrilled she almost, but not quite, felt like giving Winston a hug. Now they just had to figure out how to get the oar to Aaron and Elizabeth.

Their lifeboat was only fifteen or twenty yards away, but there was a wall of threatening waves between them. Without speaking, Jessica and Winston each grabbed an oar and began paddling furiously in Aaron and Elizabeth's direction. It was slow going. They would make some progress, and then a wave would push them back again.

Finally they were only a few yards apart. Elizabeth and Aaron clapped their hands and cheered. "Winston and Jessica to the rescue!" Elizabeth cried.

"Don't speak too soon," Winston called. He was holding the oar out at arm's length, but it still didn't quite reach. "I'm going to have to throw it to you. Here it comes!"

Winston stood up in the lifeboat. He bent his knees to brace himself, poised to toss the oar. Elizabeth and Aaron looked like baseball players ready to field a fly ball.

At that moment a swell hit Jessica and Winston's lifeboat. Winston's knees buckled, and he lost his balance. Jessica tried her hardest to steady the lifeboat, but it was no use. As Winston fell heavily to one side, the lifeboat capsized!

The last thing Jessica saw before she hit the icy water was the look of terror in Elizabeth's eyes.

She tried to hang on to the overturned lifeboat, but her hands slipped off the slick rubber. Jessica felt as helpless as a rag doll when a churning wave hit her full force and carried her away from the lifeboat.

Four

For a split second Jessica was stunned. Then the wave passed over her, and she treaded water for a minute, gasping for breath. Her eyes stinging from the salt and the driving rain, she peered around her through the fog. She couldn't see far, but all she could see was ocean. Winston, the lifeboat, and the rest of her class—Elizabeth!—were gone. Jessica was at the mercy of the waves that pushed and pulled her, drawing her farther and farther from the *Maverick*.

"Elizabeth!" Jessica cried. Another wave slapped her in the face, and she got a mouthful of seawater. She coughed. "Mr. Russo, Captain Marsden, help!"

The only answer was the roar of the wind.

Still treading water, Jessica made an effort to control her terror. She considered her situation for a moment. It wasn't good, but it could be worse. She had her life jacket on; it would keep her afloat. She had lived near the ocean all her life, and she, Elizabeth, and their older brother, Steven, had learned to swim almost as soon as they had learned to walk. Between cheerleading practice and occasionally doing laps in her family's pool, Jessica knew she was in good shape. She could swim quite a distance, if it came to that.

But which way was Anacapa Island? Which way was home? Jessica had absolutely no way of telling. The clouds had completely blackened out the sun; the fog made it impossible for her to see more than a few feet ahead of her. There was nothing by which to judge direction.

But there was a current, a strong one. Jessica realized there would be no point in swimming against it—she wouldn't make any progress.

She paused for a moment to catch her breath before starting out. There was a tight knot of fear in her stomach that she decided to ignore.

"I'm not scared," Jessica said out loud. "I'm just *mad*. Winston Egbert, you are without a doubt the world's biggest jerk. Just wait until I get to shore and get my hands on you!"

Fueled by the pleasing prospect of punishing Winston for the horrible afternoon, Jessica kicked her feet and began to swim.

It happened so quickly, Elizabeth could hardly believe her eyes. One second Jessica and Winston were securely in their lifeboat, only a few feet away from her and Aaron, and the next moment Winston had capsized the boat in the process of throwing them an oar. Aaron had reached for the flying oar and missed. But neither he nor Elizabeth really cared about the oar. They were too horror-struck at Jessica and Winston's predicament.

A tall wave rose up immediately between the two boats. When it receded, Jessica, Winston, and the empty lifeboat were nowhere in sight.

"Jessica, are you all right?" Elizabeth shrieked, gripping the edge of her lifeboat so tightly, her knuckles turned white. Her voice was tiny compared to the howl of the storm. "Winston, can you hear me? Jessica!"

Aaron yelled, too, but there was no response. "Nobody could make themselves heard above this wind," he declared. When Elizabeth was silent, Aaron turned to look more closely at her. Along with rain, her cheeks were streaked with tears. "Hey, Liz, I'm sure they're fine. They probably climbed right back into the lifeboat. They're out there," Aaron added confidently. "We just can't see them because of the fog."

Elizabeth prayed that Aaron was right. It *was* almost impossible to see. She and Aaron were having a tough time staying within view of the *Maverick*. The rest of the class was for the most part invisible. They could discern the dim shapes of only a few of the other lifeboats. *They're out there*, Elizabeth repeated silently, huddling low in the lifeboat while Aaron, wielding the one oar, did his best to keep them in the *Maverick's* vicinity. *Please let them be out there.*

Half an hour later it appeared that the storm was going to end as suddenly as it had begun. Elizabeth and Aaron noticed that the waves were gradually diminishing in size. In addition, the fog had thinned and now flowed by them in wisps rather than in a dense blanket. The driving rain had become a light drizzle.

Aaron paddled their lifeboat over to Ken and Enid, who were now visible a few yards ahead of them. "Ahoy, matie!" Aaron called cheerfully.

Ken and Enid greeted their friends with waves and smiles. Elizabeth tried her best to respond with equal enthusiasm, but she couldn't—not until she knew Jessica was safe.

The half-sunken *Maverick* had acted as home base for the lifeboats. The fog lifted to reveal them gathered in a loose circle around the *Maverick*. It was easier to paddle now that the surf was more calm, and everyone rowed their lifeboats closer toward the *Maverick*.

From his boat Bob Russo scanned the group to make a quick head count. Elizabeth craned her neck, searching for her sister. The realization came to them at the same moment: Jessica and Winston were missing.

"Where are Jessica and Winston?" Mr. Russo asked, his brow furrowed with worry. "Has anyone seen them?"

The rest of the class shook their heads. Elizabeth gulped. Her throat had gone dry, and when she opened her mouth to speak, no sound came out.

Aaron answered Mr. Russo. "The last time we saw them, their lifeboat tipped over. Winston was trying to throw me an oar. Liz and I only had one, and he had an extra. He stood up in the boat, and a big wave came and flipped the boat. Then we lost sight of them because of the fog. But they must have righted their boat. . . ."

Aaron's voice trailed off, giving away his uncertainty. Mr. Russo seemed concerned, but he didn't lose his composure. "When did this happen?"

Aaron looked at Elizabeth with a shrug. "I didn't check the time," he admitted.

Her hand shaking, Elizabeth tipped her left wrist to read her watch. "It was about half an hour ago," she said, her voice hoarse with fear. "Only a few minutes after we abandoned the *Maverick.*"

"Oh, no, they're drowned!" Lila wailed. All the students started talking at once.

Captain Marsden raised his hand to silence the crowd. "Now, kids, there's no reason to panic! By the time those two got back in their lifeboat, they'd probably drifted away from the rest of us. The best thing to do right now is look and yell. Just stay within range of the *Maverick.*" Captain Marsden turned to face Mr. Russo. "Let's pull up alongside the *Maverick.* The radio should still be working even if the engine isn't. I'll call the Coast Guard and get us picked up on the double."

Elizabeth and Aaron turned their lifeboat around and started rowing away from the char- tered boat. "Jessica!" Elizabeth shouted at the top of her lungs. "Winston!"

The rest of the group joined in the search. "Hey, Winston, you clown, I know you're out there!" Ken hollered.

"Jessica, where are you?" Lila called, her teary voice shrill.

Elizabeth yelled until her throat was sore. She strained her eyes staring out into the ocean beyond, but it was no use. As the sea calmed and the sky cleared even further, it became apparent that Jessica and Winston had really and truly disappeared.

"Oh, please be OK, Jess," Elizabeth whispered, her hands clenched tightly into fists. "Please be OK."

Suddenly there was a shout of discovery from one of the other lifeboats. Elizabeth's heart leapt. *They've found her!* she thought. *Jessica is OK!*

She and Aaron paddled quickly in the direction of Tom and Lila, who were sharing a lifeboat. Tom was leaning over the side of his boat, trying to pick something up out of the water. When he straightened up, he was holding a dripping bright-yellow life jacket.

Elizabeth stared at the life jacket, not wanting to believe her eyes.

"There was only one yellow life preserver on board," Captain Marsden informed Mr. Russo. "All the others were orange."

"Did any of you lose your life jacket?" Mr. Russo queried. "Who was wearing the yellow one?"

44

Elizabeth's vision blurred, and she found herself back on the *Maverick*, right before they had all climbed into the lifeboats. Ken Matthews, wearing an orange life jacket, had helped Jessica slip her arms into a bright yellow one. . . .

"Jessica was wearing the yellow life jacket," Elizabeth said, tears springing to her eyes.

Lila let out a wail, and Tom put his arm around her shoulders.

"Hey, wait. Here's something else!" Aaron reached behind him and grabbed something out of the ocean. Elizabeth was almost afraid to look.

It was a sodden San Diego Padres baseball hat. "Winston's," Aaron almost whispered.

Lila was sobbing in earnest now.

"Kids, we've got to remain calm," Mr. Russo urged them. "No hysterics, please. Jessica and Winston are both intelligent people, and I'm *sure* they stayed with their lifeboat."

But despite his confident words, Mr. Russo looked distraught. And everyone could hear Captain Marsden, on the radio again with the Coast Guard, loud and clear. In addition to asking for a boat to pick up the charter's stranded passengers, the captain was stressing the need for a full-scale search for two missing students.

Elizabeth sank back into the lifeboat and let

the plastic oar slip from her fingers. She had never felt so helpless in her life. She had come to Jessica's aid so many times before, on trivial occasions when Jessica had gotten herself into trouble because of some thoughtless behavior, and in times of serious danger, too. But now there was absolutely nothing Elizabeth could do. Jessica was lost at sea. Wherever she might be, Elizabeth couldn't reach her.

The fourteen remaining students pulled closer together, forming a tight knot of lifeboats along-side the chartered boat. The same look of horror, disbelief, and sorrow was on every face. Enid and Lila were both crying quietly, but Elizabeth had just gone numb.

"They'll turn up, Liz," Aaron said, mussing her still-damp hair awkwardly. "I'd say if there're two people we can count on to be able to take care of themselves, it's Winston and Jessica."

"Aaron's right," Ken agreed. "They'll turn up, in style."

But twenty minutes later, when a powerful hum heralded the arrival of a sleek Coast Guard powerboat, Jessica and Winston were still missing. One by one the students were assisted on board, followed by Mr. Russo and Captain Marsden. Then three other Coast Guard boats appeared and began their search of the area.

Elizabeth faced backward as the rescue boat swept in a wide arc across the surface of the water and then headed for the mainland. The damaged *Maverick* grew smaller and smaller until it was the size of a tiny ant on the blue horizon. Then it disappeared, swallowed up by the endless sea.

And my sister's out there somewhere, Elizabeth thought, overcome with misery. Two tears crept down her cheeks. *I hope*.

Jessica felt as if she had been swimming for three days. She could hardly feel her arms or legs anymore, she was so tired. She'd long since abandoned the crawl in favor of the breaststroke, hoping to preserve what was left of her strength for as long as possible.

At first it had taken a gigantic effort just to move through the storm-tossed sea. Foolishly she hadn't fastened the straps of her life jacket securely, and a giant wave had broken over her, tearing the loose life jacket right off her. Fortunately the waves and the wind soon died down somewhat, but as they decreased, so did Jessica's energy level. She was barely moving forward now. It was all she could do to keep her head above water.

For the first time, it struck Jessica that she might actually drown. For all she knew, she had been swimming straight out to sea, a hundred miles from anywhere! *Don't think about it,* she lectured herself. *Just swim, Wakefield!* To distract herself, she pretended she was swimming laps in the pool at home. One, two, three, four, five . . . ten . . . twenty . . . thirty-five . . . fifty . . .

Soon Jessica was too exhausted even to count. *I can't do it,* she thought despairingly. *My arms just won't move anymore!* Her strokes became slower and slower. Her eyelids dropped, and the ocean in front of her became a blur. *If I could just sleep,* Jessica thought, *just sink to the bottom of the ocean onto the soft sand and sleep. . . .*

Jessica's sight dimmed as her eyes filled with tears. She reached up quickly with one hand to rub them, straining to see in front of her. Through the fog, something dark loomed above the water. At first Jessica thought she must be dreaming. It was the sort of thing that happened to thirsty people lost in the desert. They would see a big blue lake and breeze-swept palm trees where there was only hot sand. A mirage, that was the name for it, she thought.

But, no, she wasn't dreaming! It *was* land! A little island, even smaller than Anacapa, but it would do. She was going to make it!

With all her remaining strength, Jessica stroked toward the island. When her feet touched bottom, she felt happier than she ever had before. She was still alive!

Jessica's knees were so weak that she could barely wade into shore. The waves pushed at her spaghettilike legs, knocking her forward onto the sand. Jessica was so glad to be on land that when she fell on her face on the beach, she lay that way for a minute, taking long, deep breaths and savoring the feel of solid ground beneath her. Then, her head still spinning, she sat up and looked around the beach.

She had washed up on a short area of sand backed by a thick wall of tropical greenery. Jessica tried to stand up, but her legs wouldn't support her, so she crawled. Unbelievably a ray of sunlight had sliced through the clouds. The storm was over.

Collapsing in the shade under a palm tree, Jessica fell instantly into a deep sleep.

Five

"The Coast Guard is calling off the search until
tomorrow morning," Ned Wakefield announced
in a solemn voice as he hung up the telephone.
"They can't do anything in the dark. But they
said they'll start looking again at daybreak with
helicopters as well as boats."

The family and a few close friends were gathered around the table in the Wakefields' big
Spanish-tiled kitchen. The twins' brother, Steven, a freshman at the nearby state university,
had rushed home as soon as he was told the
news. With him was Cara Walker, his girlfriend
and one of Jessica's closest friends. Elizabeth's

boyfriend, Jeffrey French, had also stopped by.

Now Jeffrey squeezed Elizabeth's hand under the table. She squeezed back to show how much she appreciated his support. She only wished she felt as brave inside as she was pretending to be on the outside.

"Well," Alice Wakefield said briskly, getting to her feet, "I guess there's not much we can do tonight, either. At least now we can stop staring at the telephone, waiting for it to ring. How about some coffee and cookies?"

Mrs. Wakefield walked over to the kitchen counter, but not before Elizabeth saw a tear running down her face. Ned Wakefield stood up and followed his wife. Putting both arms around her, he wrapped her in a tight hug.

Elizabeth's throat ached as she fought back tears of her own. She had already done enough crying that day, and she was determined to keep an optimistic attitude. But with Jessica's absence staring her in the face, it was becoming harder and harder.

After Elizabeth and the rest of the group on the ill-fated field trip had been picked up by the Coast Guard, the ride back to shore had been swift. But there had been just enough time for the story of the missing Sweet Valley High students to get out to the press. Reporters from three newspapers and two local TV stations had been waiting on the pier when the boat pulled up. Elizabeth had rushed right by them, ignoring the questions that were tossed at her and her classmates. "How well do you know the missing boy and girl?" "What kind of kids are they?" "Do you have any evidence that they're still alive?" In a dull trance Elizabeth had called her parents from a pay phone at the marina while Mr. Russo phoned the Egberts.

Now, as Elizabeth watched her mom and dad trying to cheer and comfort each other, she thought she had never seen them look so upset, so sad, so *old*, somehow.

Ned Wakefield, a senior partner for a law firm in Sweet Valley, was tall, dark-haired, and handsome. Alice Wakefield, who managed her own interior design business, was slim and blond like her daughters. They were both active, youthful people. In fact, Mrs. Wakefield was often mistaken for the twins' older sister. But tonight their faces were lined with worry, and Mr. Wakefield wasn't holding his broad shoulders as straight as usual.

A long moment of silence fell over the group.

To Elizabeth silence was even worse than the tense questions everyone had been asking her about what happened during the storm. She had to say something, just to keep herself from thinking.

Cara seemed to feel the same way. "If I know Jessica," Cara began, her dark brown eyes twinkling despite the seriousness of the situation, "she's probably hitched a ride on a passing cruise ship! I bet she's on her way home right now, lounging on the deck while the waiters bring her frosty fruit drinks."

Steven laughed uneasily. "You're right, Cara. Jessica knows how to take care of herself. Maybe it's Winston we should be worried about! Jess has probably divided the lifeboat in half—and we know whose side'll be bigger."

Elizabeth giggled. "I can just see it—Jessica reclining in the lifeboat like Cleopatra on her barge while Winston does all the rowing!"

"Whoa, there. Wait a minute!" Jeffrey held up a hand. "I'm casting my vote for Winston as king of the lifeboat. He can hold his own with Jessica any day. He'll be telling bad jokes left and right and boring her to tears with his crummy celebrity impressions!"

"He *was* driving her crazy today during the field trip," Elizabeth confirmed. "He seemed to think that because they were paired in the buddy system, they were best friends. He wouldn't leave her alone for a minute!"

Her parents returned to the table. Ned Wakefield set down a tray loaded with mugs and a steaming pot of coffee, and Alice Wakefield brought over a plate of homemade lemon squares. Everyone helped themselves, and for the first time that evening the atmosphere was somewhat relaxed. Joking about Jessica and Winston's likely battles for lifeboat supremacy had loosened them up. They fell into separate casual conversations. Cara asked about Steven's college friends, Mr. and Mrs. Wakefield discussed the problems with the filter system in the swimming pool, and Elizabeth and Jeffrey compared their latest assignments for *The Oracle*.

Then the telephone rang. Elizabeth jumped out of her chair and grabbed the wall-mounted phone in the kitchen before the second ring.

"Hello?" she said breathlessly. It just had to be the Coast Guard, calling to say they had decided to search a little longer that night and had found Jessica and Winston!

"Elizabeth? This is Lila."

Elizabeth slumped against the refrigerator, crushed with disappointment. "Hi, Lila," she said, shaking her head at her family, Cara, and Jeffrey.

"Is there any news?" Lila's voice was high and shaky. "I've been so upset!"

"No, Lila," Elizabeth informed her gently. "No news. The Coast Guard had to stop looking when it got dark. We're hoping they'll have more luck in the morning."

Lila sniffled on the other end. "I feel just terrible," she wailed.

"Me, too." Elizabeth wished Lila hadn't reminded her just *how* terrible.

"What if I never see Jessica again?" Lila asked, on the verge of hysteria again. "I've been mean to her so many times. I'll never have a chance to tell her I'm sorry!"

Elizabeth was sympathetic—Lila was Jessica's best friend, after all—but at the same time she didn't exactly feel like listening to a confession of all the catty things Lila had said and done to Jessica over the years. "Look, Lila, there's no need to feel badly," Elizabeth hurried to reassure her. "I know you and Jess have had your differences, but—"

Lila cut her off in midsentence. "All the times I've made her feel inferior because she can't afford as many expensive clothes as I can and

55

she doesn't have her own car or as much jewelry. And all the times we've fought over boys!"

Elizabeth fought the urge to hang up on Lila, who had begun sniffling even more loudly. "Lila, I promise I'll call you as soon as we hear anything," she said patiently. "Jessica wouldn't want you to be so upset. I'm sure she's stolen as many boys away from you as you've stolen from her."

That seemed to comfort Lila somewhat. "Thanks, Liz," she said, sounding more composed. "And tell your parents I hope . . . well, you know."

"I will. Bye, Lila."

Shaking her head, Elizabeth rejoined the others. Cara smiled with understanding. Lila was one of her closest friends as well. "I can imagine what Lila was babbling about." Cara tipped her head to one side, her long dark hair falling over her shoulder. "She couldn't just be unselfishly concerned about Jessica. She's probably feeling guilty, too, right?"

"Right!"

Cara laughed. "Well, underneath all that self-interest I know Lila really does care. Those two have been through a lot together."

"And they'll go through a lot more together," Steven predicted optimistically.

Everyone managed to drink some coffee and eat a few of the lemon squares. Then, at the same moment, Jeffrey and Cara both looked at the kitchen clock and got to their feet.

"I should be going, Liz," Jeffrey said. "I still have to read a couple of chapters for history before my quiz tomorrow."

"I'll drive you home," Steven told Cara, standing up.

Jeffrey shook hands silently with Mr. Wakefield while Cara gave Mrs. Wakefield a quick hug. Good-nights were exchanged, and then Elizabeth walked Jeffrey to the front door.

"I wish you could stay," she said wistfully. Elizabeth knew her parents would go to bed soon, and Steven would probably linger awhile at Cara's. She didn't want to be alone.

"So do I," Jeffrey told her. "Here, let's sit out front for a few more minutes. I'm not in that much of a hurry."

They closed the front door behind them and sat down side by side on the steps. The night was balmy. A soft breeze carried the scent of flowers and damp earth. A full moon was obscured by small, ragged clouds moving slowly across the sky.

Jeffrey put an arm around Elizabeth's shoulders and pulled her close. She felt his lips move against her hair, and the tender gesture caused tears to fill her eyes.

"I hate to leave you," Jeffrey whispered. "Will you be all right?"

"I-I guess." Elizabeth sighed. "I might as well go to bed, although I have a feeling I'm not going to sleep much tonight."

"Everything's going to turn out fine," Jeffrey promised. "Jessica knows how to handle boats and water. She'll make it. I know it, Liz."

With all her heart, Elizabeth wanted to believe Jeffrey. But she couldn't clear her mind of one persistent, devastating image. No matter how hard she tried to shake it, it kept coming back to her: Winston standing up in the lifeboat with the extra oar in his hand, leaning too far forward . . . the boat tipping wildly, then capsizing . . . Winston and Jessica hurling into the raging surf . . .

"I just feel as if I should have been able to stop it from happening," she said, thinking out loud.

"Stop what from happening?" Jeffrey asked, looking into her eyes.

"The accident," Elizabeth explained. "If Aaron hadn't forgotten the second oar, we wouldn't have needed the extra one Winston had taken. If Mr. Russo hadn't made us use the buddy system, I would have been in Winston's lifeboat instead of Jessica. Winston and I were together when the charter boat started to sink." Elizabeth's voice dropped to a choked whisper. "It's my fault Jessica's lost at sea!"

"Stop that, Liz!" Jeffrey ordered her sternly. "You know that's not true." He put a hand under her chin and looked down at her with a teasing smile. "It sounds like you let some of Lila's guilty feelings rub off on you."

Elizabeth smiled back, very weakly. "Maybe. But, Jeffrey—"

"No *buts* about it," he interrupted her. "You and everyone else on the trip did everything possible. Now it's out of your hands. The Coast Guard people know what they're doing. They'll find her."

They sat for a few more minutes in silence, and then Jeffrey stood up, pulling Elizabeth to her feet with him. He wrapped his arms around her and put his mouth on hers for a long, warm kiss. While Jeffrey was holding her, Elizabeth felt safe. There couldn't really be anything wrong with the world when they were together, she thought.

But then Jeffrey stepped away from her, and suddenly, despite the warmth of the night air, Elizabeth shivered.

"Will I see you in school tomorrow?" Jeffrey asked.

Elizabeth nodded. "My parents said I could stay home with them to wait for news, but I have a history quiz I have to take, too. Plus I still haven't finished my column for the next issue of the paper."

"I'll meet you at your locker before first period, then."

"OK. Good night, Jeffrey. Thanks for staying with me—for being here. You know."

"Anytime. Good night, Liz."

Jeffrey brushed Elizabeth's lips with one more gentle kiss, and then she watched him stride down the front walk toward his car. Before he pulled away from the curb, he rolled down the window and waved. She waved back, then opened the door and stepped into the front hallway.

The house was quiet—too quiet. Usually at ten o'clock Jessica would just be hitting her stride. While Elizabeth worked on homework at the table in her own bedroom, Jessica would be blasting the stereo in hers, at the same time talking loudly on the phone to Lila, Cara, or Amy. Elizabeth would ask her sister to turn the music down, and Jessica would do it, but then she would forget five minutes later when her favorite song came on the radio. The stereo would blast again, and this time the music would be accompanied by tapping feet as Jessica gave in to the rhythm and danced around the bedroom, pulling the phone by its cord along with her.

Elizabeth went into the living room and said good night to her parents, giving each of them an especially long hug. Then she slowly climbed the stairs. Upstairs, Elizabeth found herself pausing in front of Jessica's door.

She put her hand around the doorsill and felt for the light switch on the wall. Elizabeth turned on the overhead light and looked around her sister's room. On the spur of the moment a few years ago, Jessica had painted the walls of her bedroom a dark chocolate brown. Known by the rest of the family as "The Hershey Bar," the room was a stark contrast to Elizabeth's, which was painted a creamy off-white. And that wasn't the only difference. Jessica's room was a permanent disaster area. Pyramids of discarded clothing completely covered the carpeting, and her bed looked as if it hadn't been made in a month. The plants by her window desperately needed watering. Even the posters on her walls were falling off.

Elizabeth smiled. Jessica's personality was all over the room. Elizabeth might tease her sister about living in such a mess, but she wouldn't have seen the room any cleaner for the world.

Then Elizabeth's smile dissolved as tears threatened once again. What if her twin was really gone and this room was all she had left of Jessica?

Six

Still half asleep, Jessica lazily stretched her arms over her head and yawned. *I must have overslept,* she thought, feeling the warmth of bright sunlight on her eyelids. *Why didn't Mom or Liz wake me up? Isn't it a school day? I'm going to miss first period!*

Then Jessica felt sand underneath her. Had she fallen asleep at the beach? She forced her eyes open and blinked a few times.

She had to shield her eyes with one hand. The morning sun was incredibly bright, even for Sweet Valley. As she took in the scene around her—the waves lapping against the white sand beach, the palm tree overhead, the endless ocean, and the empty horizon—suddenly the events of the day before came back to her in a rush. She had been shipwrecked!

Curious, she sat up and looked around. It was hard to believe that the ocean had ever been rough and gray and angry. There were still a few scattered clouds, but the sky was a clear sapphire blue, its brilliant color mirrored in the smooth sea below. There were birds singing, and the fronds of the palm trees rustled in the breeze.

"This place isn't half bad!" Jessica said out loud, rubbing the sore muscles in her upper arms. "This could be kind of fun. I'm a castaway, like on *Gilligan's Island!*" Then Jessica recalled that Gilligan and his pals had been stranded on their particular island for years. Well, that couldn't happen to her. She wasn't *that* far from civilization, or was she?

Jessica stood up and stretched, then touched her toes. Her legs were stiff. The long, hard swim the previous day had really taken its toll. She felt as if she had recently completed a triathalon. To top it all off, she was absolutely starving. She was used to a big breakfast, Wakefield style: bacon and eggs, or cereal and fruit, or pancakes swimming in maple syrup. . . .

I'll just have to find something to eat, Jessica

decided matter-of-factly. She headed away from the water, toward the dense forest of palm trees and bushes. Beyond the palms Jessica could see a tangled area of bushes and fruit trees, some with berries and some with small greenish oranges. Jessica's mouth watered. At this point she didn't care what she ate, as long as it wasn't poisonous.

Jessica grimaced as she picked her way gingerly over the trunk of a fallen palm tree and into the undergrowth. The ground was prickly beneath her bare feet—she had lost her sandals when she fell overboard. The gauze shirt she had worn as a cover-up was torn in a dozen places, offering no protection whatsoever against the branches scratching her arms and neck.

A rainbow-colored bird squawked somewhere near her left ear, and Jessica jumped. She scowled at the bird and then hesitated, confused. It was as if she had suddenly entered a tropical jungle. The plants and trees were lush and thick, forming a canopy over her head that blocked out much of the sunlight. Birds chirped at her from all sides and there was a constant buzz of insect noises.

Goosebumps rapidly dotted Jessica's skin. She had no idea where she was. The island *seemed* deserted, but maybe she wasn't the only person on it. There could be headhunters, an undiscovered tribe of wild people who had been hidden away from the world for hundreds of years. When they found her, maybe they would think she was a supernatural being or something and worship her. Or maybe they would sacrifice her in some barbaric ritual. Maybe they were cannibals! Then they'd eat her!

Jessica was about to turn and sprint back to the beach when she heard a rustling in the bushes ahead of her. Her heart started pounding. *Don't be such a wimp, Wakefield!* she commanded herself. *It's probably just a harmless little animal, or a turtle, or a bird.*

If it was only a small bird, however, it was certainly doing a good imitation of Bigfoot. The rustling grew louder, and the animal started making strange, scary noises. It growled and then it whined. The bushes it was hiding in shook vigorously.

Jessica froze in her tracks. She couldn't have moved if her life depended on it.

Suddenly *it* came bounding out of the bushes, wildly waving its arms and screeching.

Jessica screamed at the top of her lungs. For one terrifying instant she was sure it was a headhunter. Then she took a closer look.

No, it was *Winston!*

Jessica's knees buckled, and she almost collapsed, she was so relieved. After falling overboard, Winston had made it to the island, too! He wasn't a cannibalistic headhunter! "Winston, you idiot, you scared me half to death!" Jessica exclaimed, too overjoyed at the sight of a familiar face to be really mad at him for scaring her.

Winston appeared as happy to see her as she was to see him. He leapt forward to give her a giant bear hug. "Jessica, buddy! I never thought I'd see you, or anyone, ever again! I'm so glad you're all right."

Now that she was no longer in fear of her life, Jessica was just a little peeved. Of all the people to be washed up with on a romantic desert island, she had to get stuck with Winston Egbert, possibly the most annoying person she knew. Why couldn't Ken Matthews have popped out of the bushes at her? Instead it was Winston, looking more pathetic than usual in his bedraggled, shipwrecked state. Still, Winston was better than nobody, Jessica figured.

"How did you get here, anyway?" she asked Winston, "Did you swim, like me?"

"No." Winston shook his head. "I rowed here."

"You *rowed* here?"

"Yeah. After we capsized, I managed to grab

the lifeboat and one of the oars," Winston explained, sounding proud of himself. "I turned it right-side up again and looked all over for you, but by then you'd disappeared. So I just rowed—and rowed—and rowed." He shrugged. "And I landed here."

The lifeboat! Jessica was so excited, she embraced Winston. "We can get home!" she squealed. "It can't be that far to the mainland. C'mon, let's get going right now!"

"Wait a minute, Jess. I *had* the lifeboat. . . . Well, I guess I didn't pull it up high enough on the beach last night after I landed, and, um, it was gone when I woke up this morning. It must have floated away at high tide." Winston shrugged. "Sorry."

Jessica's hopes were dashed as quickly as they had risen. She wasn't glad to see Winston any longer. She was furious.

"Winston Egbert, I wish you'd never been born!" Jessica yelled, her hands on her hips. "It was all your fault our boat capsized and we got separated from everyone else in the first place. It's your fault we're stuck on this stupid island. If it wasn't for you, I'd be home with my family right now! I hope the cannibals get you. I never want to talk to you again!"

Heedless of the bushes scratching her feet

and legs, Jessica sharply turned her back on Winston and stomped off in the direction of the beach.

Winston hurried after her. "I'm sorry, Jessica," he called in a humble voice. "I know it's my fault we're stranded here. But, hey, I can make it up to you. Come over here!"

Jessica turned reluctantly. She wasn't going to *talk* to Winston, but she supposed she could *look* at him now and then. She saw him striding eagerly to the opposite end of the beach, and she followed slowly, dragging her feet. There was no reason to hurry, that was for sure.

"Look, Jess!" Winston waved his arm proudly at a flat rock piled high with oranges, berries, and a couple of silvery still-wet fish. "I woke up early this morning and picked the fruit," Winston explained. "Then I caught the fish. They swam right up to the edge of the beach. I didn't even need a rod and line!"

Jessica shrugged, pretending she wasn't impressed. "I can catch my own fish," she said pointedly.

Winston didn't seem to have heard her. "And look at this!" He knelt down next to a stack of branches enclosed in a circle of small rocks. "I was just about to start a fire. I went into the woods to find some more firewood, and that's when I saw you. I'm going to fry up this fish and have a genuine feasteroo. There's enough for both of us."

Jessica laughed scornfully. "Oh, and just how are you planning to light a fire?" she challenged. "I suppose you're going to rub two sticks together like a caveman!"

"Wrong-o," Winston corrected her, his expression triumphant. "I happen to have saved the little waterproof emergency package that was zipped in the pocket inside the lifeboat. It's got everything! Band-Aids, a Swiss army knife, *matches* . . ."

With a humph, Jessica turned her back on Winston again and marched to the other end of the beach. She sat down on the sand with her back against a log and tipped her face to the sun.

Winston acts like he's almost glad we're shipwrecked, Jessica thought, disgusted. *He's too stupid even to know when he's in trouble!*

An image of juicy berries and fresh, hot fish popped into Jessica's head, but she tried to ignore it. She didn't want to have anything to do with Winston *or* his poor excuse for breakfast. Winston was a pest, a nerd, an all-around major-league bozo. He couldn't do anything right. He'd probably burn the fish and feed her poisonous berries. *No*, Jessica told herself, *I'm better off on my own.*

Elizabeth chewed her ham-and-cheese sandwich without even tasting it, oblivious of the usual lunchtime commotion around her in the cafeteria. She was only vaguely aware of voices and laughter, the clink of glasses and silverware, the scraping of chairs.

All morning at school she had been trying her best to concentrate, and failing miserably. She probably should have stayed home as her mother and father had suggested. She'd blanked out on her history quiz, something that had never happened to her before. She would probably get an F—that would be a first, too. But Elizabeth found it hard to care. She felt as if half of her mind and heart and soul were missing, and she knew she would keep feeling that way until Jessica was found.

"I hate to see such good food go to waste," Jeffrey teased as Elizabeth pulled a plastic bag of homemade oatmeal-raisin cookies out of her lunch bag and then pushed them away.

Elizabeth forced a smile for Jeffrey's benefit. She knew how hard he was trying to cheer her up. "They're all yours," she offered. Jeffrey took a cookie and munched it with a satisfied expression.

"Here come some more sympathizers, Liz," Enid warned Elizabeth.

Elizabeth looked up from the table with a resigned sigh. All morning long, people had been staring at her, in her classes and in the halls. She knew they weren't just curious stares—she knew the other students felt for her and what she must be going through—but still it made her skin crawl. It was as if people were already thinking, "There goes Elizabeth Wakefield, the girl whose twin sister was drowned during that science class field trip."

But Jessica hasn't drowned, Elizabeth reminded herself. *It's just going to take the Coast Guard awhile to locate them. There's a lot of water out there, and Jessica and Winston are in a tiny lifeboat.*

Elizabeth, Enid, and Jeffrey had chosen an out-of-the-way corner table in the lunchroom because Elizabeth hadn't felt much like socializing. But they had been spotted anyway, and as Enid observed, the gang was trooping over: Cara, Amy Sutton, Ken, Aaron, Robin Wilson, and Bruce Patman. Once everyone had pulled up a chair, there was quite a crowd around the small table.

Robin Wilson, who was co-captain of the cheerleading squad with Jessica, was the first to speak. "Liz, I don't know what to say," she began, giving Elizabeth's hand an awkward pat. "I'm going crazy worrying about Jess and Winston. I can imagine how you must feel!"

"It's no picnic," Elizabeth said with a feeble attempt at lightheartedness.

Even wealthy, arrogant Bruce Patman was wearing a solemn expression. "It shouldn't have happened," he declared with the confidence of someone whose family owned a whole fleet of yachts. "Obviously that charter boat wasn't seaworthy."

"It was an accident," Ken assured him. "I know something about boats, and I think it could have happened to any boat. The waves and the wind were just tearing the thing apart."

"I just can't believe it," said Amy Sutton. "I almost went on that field trip. I'm so lucky I didn't! I could be out there with Jessica in the middle of the Pacific Ocean right now." She shivered.

Elizabeth shook her head. *Trust Amy to worry about herself instead of one of her best friends*, she thought. She wished they would change the conversation to something else. But she understood that talking about Jessica and Winston helped ease the tension everyone was feeling.

73

"It's pretty freaky," Ken agreed. "It all happened so fast. I was talking to Jessica right before we had to jump ship." He smiled, remembering. "She was being lively and funny, her typical self. And then"—he lifted his broad shoulders in a helpless gesture—"she was gone."

"It's just not the same without them around," Aaron observed. "That crazy Winston! He was always up to something."

"Yeah," Bruce added, "something *dumb*!"

Aaron laughed. "That's true. We were always getting on his case for being such a goof."

There was a moment of thoughtful silence.

"We teased him something awful, didn't we?" said Cara.

"Maybe we gave him *too* hard a time now and then," Ken agreed, frowning. "I know I for one could be pretty mean."

"Me, too." Looking guilty, Bruce ran a hand through his dark hair. "It was just so easy to harass Egbert. He was such a perfect target!"

"I guess there's no point in beating ourselves over the head about it now," Aaron said. "It's too late to go back and treat him better."

Elizabeth had been playing distractedly with the gold lavaliere that hung on a delicate chain around her neck. It had been a sixteenth-birthday present from her parents, and Jessica wore an

74

identical one. "You guys are so depressing!" Elizabeth exclaimed. "You sound like you're at a funeral or something! I think it's a little premature to be mourning. I bet at this very moment the Coast Guard is rescuing Jessica and Winston!"

Bruce, Aaron, and the others exchanged nervous glances. There was another long silence.

"What's the matter?" Jeffrey asked, looking to his best friend, Aaron, for an answer.

Aaron raised his eyebrows. "Didn't you hear?"

Aaron sounded so serious that Elizabeth felt her stomach turn over once or twice as she anticipated his next words.

"Hear what?" Jeffrey demanded urgently.

Aaron shifted awkwardly in his chair. "We were talking with Maria Santelli before we came over here. She had just been on the phone with Winston's parents. I guess the Coast Guard contacted the Egberts and probably your parents, too, Liz." He cleared his throat. "They found a lifeboat that they think was Jessica and Winston's drifting around somewhere off the coast, but no Jessica and Winston."

Enid gasped, horrified. Jeffrey put his arm around Elizabeth, who collapsed limply against him. "You're *sure* that's what they said?" Jeffrey asked, hoping the others had gotten the story wrong. But they all nodded unhappily.

For a few seconds Elizabeth felt as if she had been punched in the stomach—she couldn't get any air. Then she took a deep breath, pulling herself together with a gigantic effort. The others might be ready to give up on Jessica and Winston, but she wasn't.

"That doesn't mean anything," she argued. "There are a whole bunch of little islands out in the Pacific around Anacapa Island. The helicopters were going to check them out, too. I bet Jessica and Winston landed on one of them."

A few people nodded in encouragement. No one wanted to challenge Elizabeth's hopes. But they all knew that with every hour that went by, the odds were getting worse that Jessica and Winston would be found alive.

Seven

As Jessica stalked off in a melodramatic rage, Winston pretended to wash his hands of her. "Well, if that's the way she wants it," he said to himself nonchalantly, loud enough for Jessica to hear him. "There's enough food here for two people. Oh, well. I guess I'll just have to eat it all myself!"

Whistling cheerfully, Winston went ahead and kindled his cooking fire. He had a feeling Jessica would come crawling back once the fish was frying, and that was fine with him. His feelings hadn't really been hurt by her tantrum. He was familiar with Jessica's hotheaded style, and it was natural for her to be upset about being shipwrecked. He could have predicted that she would react the way she did, especially to his news about losing the lifeboat. Winston had to admit he deserved to be yelled at for that.

He loudly whistled a tuneless rendition of the Sweet Valley High fight song as he cleaned the fish with the Swiss army knife and then wrapped the fillets in palm leaves and laid them on the fire. After a while a tantalizing aroma wafted up from the grilled fish, and Winston's mouth watered in anticipation. It felt like a hundred years since his last meal, a lousy peanut-butter-and-jelly sandwich he'd wolfed down right before the field trip. Out of the corner of his eye he could see Jessica, about twenty yards away, perched on a log. She was wrinkling her nose, shifting the air discreetly. It was time to start the show.

Humming energetically, Winston flipped the palm-wrapped fish with a flourish. Then he sat down on the sand next to his pile of fruit and surveyed it. "Hmm, it all looks so good, I'm not sure where to start," he said loudly. He selected a large orange first and peeled it. It was unbelievably juicy, and he ate it, section by section, licking his lips dramatically. Next he sampled some plump berries, rubbing his stomach to indicate his enjoyment. At this rate he figured Jessica would be able to hold out for about a minute longer, tops.

Not even pretending to sunbathe anymore, Jessica watched Winston devour his fruit. An orange had never looked so good to her, and the smell of the fish was irresistible. She was in agony.

I swore I'd never speak to him again, Jessica reminded herself. Then she saw a loophole. She hadn't sworn she wouldn't *eat* with him, had she? And she had to eat; she had to keep up her strength. If she didn't, she would starve to death and never get off the island and away from Winston.

Standing up, Jessica casually meandered over toward Winston. "I decided to take pity on you," she informed him in a lofty tone as she approached. "It's obvious by the particularly weird way you're acting that you'll totally crack up if you're left to yourself for much longer."

"Well, thanks for saving me from insanity," Winston said amiably. "Pull up a stone and have some chow."

Jessica sat down next to Winston, grateful in spite of herself. She knew Winston saw right through her feeble excuse for giving in and coming over, but he didn't give her a hard time about it. He was willing to share his food with her, even after all the nasty things she had said to him. Jessica had to admit that she herself would have behaved differently. She probably would have hoarded her food with a vengeance and really made Winston suffer. But he was being so nice!

"Thanks," Jessica said as she helped herself to a handful of berries. At first she tried to eat in a slow, polite fashion, but it was impossible. Cramming as many berries into her mouth as she could, she reached for more. She was *so* hungry.

A minute later Winston decided the fish was done. He carefully lifted the fillets from the fire and rested them on the rock that served as their table. "One for you and one for me," he said, rubbing his hands together. "Dig in!"

Jessica unwrapped her portion and tasted the fish. It was hot, tender, and delicious. "My compliments to the chef," she said to Winston as she took another bite.

Winston made a comical half bow. "I'm so glad madam is pleased with my little concoction. It's an old family recipe."

The fish disappeared in a matter of seconds. Winston licked his fingers, and Jessica wiped her mouth delicately on a palm leaf. "Thanks again, Winston. I mean, for sharing your food with me," Jessica said. "How can I repay you?" Her turquoise eyes sparkled mischievously. "I know, I'll do the dishes!"

Jessica made a great fuss of collecting the charred palm leaves and dumping them in the bushes. She dusted off the rock they had eaten on with a fern frond and buried the orange peels in the sand. "This is kind of fun," she admitted. "It sure beats *real* housework, anyway."

Winston bit into another orange while Jessica settled herself down on the sand nearby. Now that she had eaten, she felt a lot more upbeat about her—their—predicament. It probably would be only a matter of minutes before a huge rescue boat pulled up at the island. Her parents and Liz and Steve would be on board, as well as Ken Matthews, and perhaps even the mayor of Sweet Valley. There would be tears of joy and lots of picture taking. Winston would describe how they had caught and cooked the fish, and everyone would marvel at their ability to survive under such primitive conditions. A statewide holiday would be declared and a ticker-tape parade held in their honor . . .

Jessica's eyelids drooped. The sun had climbed higher while she and Winston ate. It was now at the perfect angle for tanning. Jessica smiled to herself, imagining how her friends, Lila especially, would envy her. Maybe she was stranded with Winston and not some gorgeous hunk, but she was still missing a day of school and lounging on a tropical beach. And after she was rescued, she would be a celebrity.

Jessica's daydreams were interrupted when a shadow came between her and the sun. A cloud? she wondered, opening one eye. But it was Winston, standing over her with a purposeful expression on his face. Jessica frowned as all the irritating incidents on the field trip with her *buddy* came back to her. She should have known it would be just a matter of time before Winston disturbed her peace.

"Up and at 'em!" Winston urged, sounding like an army drill sergeant. "No sleeping on the job, Jessica. We have work to do!"

"*Work?*" Jessica stared at him, shielding her eyes with her hand. "Winston, don't tell me the sun's already gotten to you. In case you haven't noticed, we're stranded on an island in the middle of the Pacific Ocean. It's a gorgeous day. The word *work* just does not apply in this situation!"

"That's where you're wrong." Winston didn't appear to be the least bit taken aback by Jessica's sharp tone. "You want to be rescued, don't you?"

"Of course!"

"And if we're not rescued right away, you want to have food and shelter, don't you?"

Jessica hated to admit it, but what Winston said made sense. "I guess," she acknowledged grudgingly. She sighed and slowly got to her feet. "You're right. Where do we start?"

Winston slapped her on the shoulder. "That's the team spirit!" he commended her. "First we need to make some kind of sign to attract rescuers. This little beach is a good spot. It's visible from the water and from the sky."

"I know what you mean!" Jessica exclaimed. "In the movies, people on deserted islands always write messages in the sand, making big letters out of sticks and leaves and stuff." That sounded like a great idea to Jessica. She could do it and work on her tan at the same time.

But Winston greeted her suggestion with a dismissive wave of his hand. "That would take hours," he pointed out. "It wouldn't be an efficient use of our time and energy. What *I* had in mind was to find a bright object to use as a reflector. Something that'll catch the sunlight. We could send S.O.S. signals with it."

"OK." Jessica shrugged. "I don't care, to tell

you the truth. But where are you going to find a bright object?"

"Well . . ." Winston hesitated. His eyes fastened on Jessica's right wrist.

"Oh, no, you don't." She put her left hand protectively over her wide bracelet. "This happens to be fourteen-karat gold. My grandmother gave it to me."

"We won't lose it," Winston argued. "I promise you. C'mon, fork it over!"

"Make me." Jessica crossed her arms over her chest and faced Winston with her best stone-faced scowl.

"Jessica, be reasonable!" For a moment Winston sounded uncharacteristically serious. "I'm only trying to help. I want to get us off this island as quickly as possible. A reflector would be much more effective than letters in the sand. I'm not just asking for your bracelet so I can play a game with it. This is survival!"

Winston's sincere efforts to save them made Jessica feel embarrassed about the selfish way she had reacted to the suggestion. She supposed he *was* only trying to get things done. But, still, there was no way she was going to let that bracelet leave her wrist.

"You're right, a reflector probably is a better idea than writing in the sand," Jessica conceded.

"But you're going to have to find some other bright object."

Winston's eyes lit up. "And I just thought of something else we can use, thank you very much!" he announced. "The Swiss army knife!"

Jessica was relieved that she wouldn't have to worry about holding on to her bracelet. "Great!"

Winston trotted off to get the knife. Jessica stood on the beach looking out over the water, her eyes narrowed against the bright sun. It was such a big sky and such a huge ocean. How was anybody going to see their measly little pocketknife?

Suddenly Jessica felt very small and very lost. But before she had a chance to feel sorry for herself, Winston rejoined her, carrying the knife and a rock to rest it on. "Periodically we can spend a few minutes flashing it. The rest of the time we can just leave it here," he told Jessica. "A stationary reflection's better than none." He busied himself positioning the knife.

Jessica would never have admitted it to anyone, but it was really kind of nice to have Winston around. It was definitely an improvement over being alone, anyway. Jessica knew she would have been a lot more scared, and a lot hungrier, if she hadn't stumbled upon Winston.

He was actually taking charge of the situation, in his own oddball fashion. It would never have occurred to her to have devised some sort of signal to passing boats and planes. Thanks to Winston, the two of them might get off the island soon, and in the meantime, she was well fed and she had someone to talk to.

Relaxing somewhat, Jessica sat down on the sand. *Maybe Winston Egbert's not so bad after all!* she thought.

Eight

"Hey, Winston!" Jessica called. "When are you serving lunch?"

Winston, who had wandered off to explore the island, had just reappeared at the opposite end of the beach from where Jessica was sunbathing. He joined her and squatted in the sand.

"Don't tell me you're hungry again already!" He feigned amazement. "I know you're energetic, Jess, but I didn't know you had to eat every hour on the hour."

Jessica slapped Winston playfully on the shoulder. "It's been a whole *bunch* of hours since that fish," she corrected him in self-defense. "And admit it, you've got to be starving after all your exploring."

"Why, yes, I am rather famished," Winston confessed in a self-important tone. "It was rough going, navigating such uncharted terrain."

"Well, what did Lewis and Clark and Egbert discover out there?" Jessica teased.

Winston settled onto the sand, sitting cross-legged. "It's a good-sized island," he reported. "I think I only made it about a third or fourth of the way around the perimeter. I pretty much stayed to the beach because it was easier walking. But I found a stream for drinking water and a little bluff that drops in a cliff right down to the ocean. And lots of palm trees."

"I don't suppose you saw a hot dog stand or an ice-cream parlor," Jessica said wistfully.

Winston shook his head. "Nope. But I saw tons more berries and fruit, and we know that beautiful ocean out there is just hopping with fish!"

Jessica wrinkled her nose. She had a feeling she could get tired of a berry and fish diet awfully fast. On the other hand, maybe she should ignore her hunger pangs and try to lose some weight. Then, when she bent back to school after being rescued, she would be slimmer as well as more tanned. Ken Matthews would fall over when he saw her.

"But when *are* we going to be rescued?" Jessica worried out loud. A couple of jet planes had flown over the island that morning, probably on their way to Hawaii, but for the most part, both the sea and the sky had remained empty.

Winston shrugged. "It's impossible to tell," he said. "I suppose it could be hours—or it could be days. That's why I think we should go right now and find some food. But not just for lunch today. I think we should make a little stockpile. Then every time we need to eat we don't have to go hunting and foraging."

Jessica wriggled her toes in the sand. Gathering berries just didn't sound like much fun to her. And if they *were* rescued in a matter of hours rather than days, all that labor would be pointless.

"You can go ahead and look for food," Jessica informed him. "I think I'll just pick some flowers and decorate my end of the beach."

Winston shook his head. "No, we've got to work as a team, Jessica," he insisted. "Teamwork's essential to wilderness survival, and finding food before nightfall is our number-one priority."

Jessica rolled her eyes. "Give me a break, Egbert. You sound like a Cub Scout leader! I mean, really, finding food won't take much time at all. We can do it later. I want to do something *fun*." Jessica had a vision of herself wearing a skirt made of palm fronds and with pink hibiscus woven in her loose, flowing hair. She would be reclining against a bower of fragrant tropical flowers when the rescue boat pulled up. One thing was for sure, she couldn't greet any handsome sailors looking like she did right now. Her shorts and shirt were wrinkled beyond belief, not to mention being torn and full of sand. Her hair was one big tangle. Improving her appearance was *her* top priority.

"*Fun?*" Winston pronounced the word as if he'd never heard it before, which Jessica found amusing, considering he was always kidding around.

"Yes," Jessica said. "Fun. Got something against it?"

"Nope." Winston's expression remained self-righteous. "But there's a time and place for everything."

He turned away from Jessica to look out at the water and the sky. She followed his gaze. The sky had become partly cloudy, and the northwesterly breeze had picked up quite a bit since that morning. "It looks like rain to me," Winston speculated. "What do you think?"

"Maybe," Jessica admitted. "But I'm not a meteorologist," she added dryly.

"Well, I think we should wait on the food and build a shelter instead, right away. *And* collect some firewood and get it under cover where it'll stay dry," Winston suggested.

To Jessica that sounded even more uninteresting than gathering food. "Do we have to?" She moaned.

"Do you want to get soaking wet and freeze to death—and be starving on top of that?" Winston challenged her.

Jessica stuck her tongue out at him. "I plan to be rescued before it starts to rain," she informed him airily.

Winston sighed. "Women," he muttered under his breath. Then he held up one index finger, inspired. "I know, how about this? We'll build a shelter together, and *then* you can pick your flowers and decorate it. That way it'll be half work and half fun. Is that a fair compromise?"

Jessica pretended to hold out, for the sake of argument. But inside she knew that Winston's proposal was sensible. She didn't want to get caught in the rain. Then she would look even worse when the rescuers arrived! "OK," she relented. "I'll help you build the stupid shelter. Anything to get you off my back!"

"I knew you'd come around to my way of thinking sooner or later," Winston said. "You've got what it takes to be an Eagle Scout, Wakefield."

"Don't press your luck, Egbert!" Jessica warned him, standing up and dusting the sand off her shorts.

They decided to build the shelter on the north side of the beach where Winston had lit the fire that morning. A tall heap of rocks created a natural back wall. "We'll only need two front supports—a couple of long, sturdy branches or lightweight logs—and then we'll be able to put up a roof," Winston declared.

That sounded easy enough to Jessica. "You're the boss," she reminded Winston. "I'm ready to take my orders!"

"No, we're equals," he said. "A team, remember?"

Jessica rolled her eyes. "All right, *team*mate. But you're still going to have to tell me what to do. I don't take shop, remember?"

Winston chuckled.

They started by scouring the woods for two fallen branches big enough to act as pillars to support the front end of the shelter. It didn't take long to find them; there were dozens of fallen trees scattered in the forest beyond the beach. "Mark this spot, Jess," Winston recommended. "We should come back here to get some firewood later."

"Yes, sir," Jessica joked.

Next they collected lighter, more flexible branches to lay on top of the wooden supports. They connected them to the stone wall in the back and threaded them through each other, thereby forming the base for a roof. Winston used some of the string from the emergency kit to tie branches snugly together. The final step was to gather palm leaves, lots of them. Layers of the large, thick leaves stitched roughly onto branches with string almost magically became side walls for the shelter. When they layered palm leaves on top for the roof as well, the shelter was complete.

Both Jessica and Winston were thrilled with the product of their labor. Jessica clapped her hands, delighted. "It's so rustic, just like something out of a movie!" she exclaimed.

"Not a bad piece of construction," Winston admitted proudly.

"And I have a few ideas for the inside," Jessica said.

"While you're working on that, I'll build a

fire pit with stones outside the open end of the shelter," Winston told her.

The first thing Jessica did was gather yet another armful of palm fronds. Spreading them across the sand at the rear of the shelter, she created a sort of palm-leaf sofa. Then she located some leafy vines she had noticed earlier and cut a few dozen pieces of the vine to hang from the roof to the floor of the shelter. She used these to create a curtain that separated the shelter into two rooms, one for her and one for Winston. Last but not least she picked a whole bunch of fresh, fragrant flowers to fill the corners of the shelter and the cracks in the rock wall.

"I'm beat!" Jessica announced after she had placed her last flower in their new cottage. She sat down on the sofa on her side of the vine curtain and stretched out her legs.

Winston had just finished the fire pit, and now he ducked inside the four-foot-high shelter. He whistled his appreciation of Jessica's work. "Wow, this is wild!" he enthused. "Kind of primitive, kind of psychedelic. I'll bet they feature this in the next issue of *Good Housekeeping*."

Jessica shrugged. "What can I say? My mom's an interior designer. I guess that's where my exquisite taste comes from!" She giggled, picturing her bedroom at home with its brown walls, dying plants, and eternal mess. Now *that* was a room for *Good Housekeeping!*

"Well . . ." Winston put his hands in the pockets of his khaki shorts. "May I join you?" he asked formally.

"Of course!" Jessica moved over to make room for Winston on the sofa.

He sat down gingerly, careful not to disturb the neatly arranged fronds. They sat for a few minutes in companionable silence, surveying their work. The sandy floor was smooth and soft. The palm-leaf sides and roof were tightly woven, and sunlight filtered in through only a few small holes. If it rained, they would probably stay fairly dry.

"It looks pretty nice, huh?" Winston glanced at Jessica for confirmation.

"Oh, yeah. All the comforts of home," she agreed. "Well, some of them, anyway."

"And that's thanks to you," Winston said shyly. "I, um, admire the way you pitched in with this and worked so hard decorating and stuff. It really makes a difference. I couldn't have done all this on my own."

"You sound surprised!" Jessica noted, not sure whether to feel flattered or offended, but leaning toward the latter.

"Well, let's just put it this way," Winston began. "I think I've seen a new side of you since we've been here on this island. I mean, not that your other sides are so bad, but—" He made a wry face. "I'm putting my foot in my mouth, huh?"

"A couple of toes, at least," Jessica said. Under any other circumstances she really would have gotten steamed and told Winston just what she thought of him. But in the time they had spent on the island together, things between them had changed a little. She thought she knew what Winston was trying to say, in his usual tactless way. She couldn't believe it, but Winston had surprised her, too. If she had been stuck on the island on her own, she would still be frying herself in the sun, not giving a thought to food and shelter.

"I guess I know what you mean," Jessica added grudgingly, a moment later. She smoothed the sandy floor with one hand. "I would never have thought a practical joker like you could be so practical!"

She looked at Winston and grinned. He blushed and Jessica lowered her eyes, feeling stupid. *How can you even think such sappy things about Winston Egbert, of all people?* she wondered to herself. Maybe she had lost her mind during that long swim to the island. Maybe she was just in shock. In any case, she thought she had better stop talking. Winston might get ideas, imagine she actually wanted to be *friends* with him.

Winston broke the awkward pause first by jumping abruptly to his feet. "We probably shouldn't waste time sitting around," he said, getting back to the business at hand. "We still need food and firewood. Ready for action?"

Jessica jumped up from the couch and raced to the door of the shelter, happy to have an excuse to cut their conversation short. "Last one to catch a fish is a rotten egg!" she yelled as she ran toward the beach ahead of him.

Nine

"I just can't sit here doing nothing any longer!" Steven declared, his brown eyes filled with frustration.

Elizabeth flashed her brother a sympathetic look. She knew exactly how he was feeling. She'd had about all the waiting she could take, too.

She had driven home right after school, having managed to finish her column for *The Oracle* during her free period. It was probably the worst one she had ever written, but at least it was done.

Steven and her parents were in the kitchen, in practically the same positions they had occupied the night before. The Coast Guard was still looking for Jessica and Winston, using boats and helicopters, and the Wakefield and Egbert families couldn't do anything but sit by the phone and wait for the latest report from the search team.

Mr. Wakefield put a hand on his son's shoulder. "It's tough not being able to take any action ourselves," he agreed. "We just have to be patient."

"But we *could* take action ourselves," Elizabeth spoke up. Her family looked at her, obviously startled by her suggestion. "I bumped into Bruce Patman in the hall after the last bell," she explained. "He'd just called Nicholas Morrow at work." Nicholas, already a high school graduate, was taking time off before college to work in his father's computer company. "Bruce and Nicholas started talking about Jessica and Winston, and Nicholas offered to take a group of us out in his family's boat to look for them."

"Do you think that's a good idea, Ned? Do you think it's safe?" Alice Wakefield anxiously asked her husband.

"Oh, Mom, you know Nicholas!" Elizabeth said quickly, before her father could respond. "He's a very experienced sailor. He races his own sailboat single-handedly. And he's very mature and responsible."

"Well . . ." Mr. Wakefield loosened the knot on his tie as he thought about the suggestion. "I don't see why not, Alice. There won't be any trouble with Nicholas at the helm. The weather's perfect, besides."

"Good, then I'll call him right now!" Elizabeth hurried to the telephone, glad to have something to do.

"Way to go, Liz!" Steven cheered.

Elizabeth reached Nicholas at his office. He had already arranged to take the rest of the afternoon off, and he was glad the Wakefields had decided to take him up on his offer.

"He said he'll meet us at the marina in half an hour," Elizabeth informed Steven. "Bruce and Ken are going to come along, and Nicholas says there's plenty of room for Cara and Jeffrey, too. Can we borrow your car, Dad?"

"Sure. Good luck!" Mr. Wakefield encouraged them. "I hope you find her, but be careful."

Steven was already halfway to the door. "Let's go!"

Elizabeth and Steven picked up Cara and Jeffrey on the way to the marina. Nicholas, Bruce, and Ken, all dressed in shorts and T-shirts, and wearing sunglasses, were already gathered at the pier where the Morrows' yacht was berthed.

As she strode down the weathered wooden ramp, Elizabeth experienced a sensation of déjà vu that sent a shiver up her spine. Was it really only yesterday that she and Jessica had arrived at the marina, just in time to board the *Maverick* and head off on the field trip? It seemed like years had elapsed since then.

Now Elizabeth felt a qualm on her own behalf. The wind down by the water was very brisk, and whitecaps dotted the ocean. Even though the sky was clear, there were a few dark clouds on the horizon, far, far away. She didn't really want to get on another boat after what she'd gone through the day before. *You chicken!* she accused herself. *You'll be perfectly safe with Nicholas in charge. And Jessica's life is at stake!*

Elizabeth felt braver when Jeffrey took her hand and gave it a warm squeeze, as if he knew what she was thinking.

Nicholas greeted Elizabeth with a brotherly hug. "I can imagine what you guys are going through," he said as he shook Steven's hand firmly. His voice was rough with emotion, and Elizabeth knew he was thinking about his own sister, Regina, who had died recently.

"Thank you so much for helping us look for Jessica and Winston," Elizabeth said softly.

Nicholas squeezed her shoulder with one strong hand. "It's the least I can do."

A minute later the entire group had boarded the twenty-eight-foot *Nighthawk*. While Nicholas started the powerful engine, the others removed the tarps. Within five minutes they were chugging out of the harbor. Nicholas carefully obeyed the harbor speed limit until he reached the buoys marking the harbor mouth, and then he gunned the engine, and the *Nighthawk* really took off.

Ken spread out a nautical map of the area. Bruce took the wheel while Nicholas conferred with Ken about the best possible course to take.

"Judging by the direction of the storm yesterday, I think we should head for the southernmost Channel Islands," Ken recommended. "We were only fifteen minutes from Anacapa Island when we jumped ship and Jess and Winston disappeared. They might have made it back to Anacapa or another one of these little islands." He pointed them out on the map.

"It looks like a logical place to start," Nicholas agreed. "Hey, Patman!" he yelled as the *Nighthawk* began speeding even faster. "What are you trying to do with my boat, fly it?"

Bruce looked over his shoulder, his hair whipping in the wind, and grinned. "I happen to know for a fact that Jessica Wakefield doesn't like to be kept waiting!" he retorted.

Pretending to be peeved, Nicholas took over the wheel. From where she was sitting, snuggled securely next to Jeffrey, Elizabeth watched Nicholas. His strong profile—the dark hair, straight nose, and determined expression—and his take-charge attitude filled her with hope. And Bruce's flip remark had lightened her heart. Bruce spoke as if Jessica were just over the curve of the horizon, standing on the shore of one of the islands, tapping her foot impatiently. It was a welcome change from the way the gang had been talking earlier in the day during lunch period.

Elizabeth took a deep breath of the crisp, salty air. "We're going to find them," she told Jeffrey confidently. "I just have a feeling!"

Jeffrey pulled her closer to him, his eyes taking on some of the enthusiasm in her own. "That's the spirit, Liz!"

Soon they neared the spot where Ken thought the *Maverick* had foundered. As Nicholas swung the *Nighthawk* in a broad arc, setting a course for the islands Ken had pinpointed on the map, the others took up posts along the yacht's railings. Steven, Cara, and Bruce looked off the starboard side while Elizabeth, Jeffrey, and Ken covered the port. They weren't looking for a lifeboat anymore, but they were hoping to spot some other evidence—a piece of clothing, for instance.

"A message in a bottle would be nice," Ken joked.

They were still a couple of miles from the first of the Channel Islands when the rain began. First it fell in large, solitary drops, then it grew to a steady downpour. The dark clouds that had been hovering on the horizon when they started out from the marina were now looming overhead.

Nicholas frowned. "I don't like this weather," he admitted, "but it shouldn't slow us down. The *Nighthawk*'s seen worse. We keep a bunch of raincoats in that box over there. Help yourselves."

Ken caught Elizabeth's eye. "I don't like this weather, either," he said in a low voice. "It's too much like the weather yesterday."

"Oh, I don't know," Elizabeth said. "I'm sure it's just a passing shower," she commented with a casual wave of her hand. The truth was, the butterflies had started up in her stomach, too, but she didn't want to panic, not now when they had a chance of finding Jessica and Winston.

Just then a spidery streak of lightning flickered across the sky. Only seconds later the ear-splitting boom of a thunderclap made them all jump.

Nicholas was listening to the ship-to-shore radio, and now he slapped his hand against the wheel. "Of all the luck!" he exclaimed.

"What is it?" Ken asked, moving closer so he could hear the radio, too.

The message that had caught Nicholas's attention was repeated on the radio, punctuated by sharp bursts of static. It was an all-craft warning to return to shore. Another storm was approaching, one that promised to be as severe as that of the previous day.

No one, not even a bitterly disappointed Elizabeth, argued with Nicholas as he made a U-turn and headed back toward the coast. If it wasn't safe to be on the water, they had no choice but to abandon their search.

After dropping off their friends, Steven and Elizabeth headed straight home. Steven tried to look at the bright side. "Well, at least we got out of the house for a while. We killed some time."

"Yes. That's true." Elizabeth stared out the car window at the driving rain. Jessica and Winston were out there somewhere in this storm, alone and unprotected.

To Elizabeth and Steven's surprise, when they

pulled into the driveway their parents were standing in the front doorway, as if they'd been watching for them to return.

"We were worried to death!" Mrs. Wakefield cried as Elizabeth and Steven climbed out of the car. She looked mad, upset, and relieved all at the same time.

"About fifteen minutes after you left we heard on the radio that there was a bad storm coming," Mr. Wakefield explained, his own relief apparent. "They were telling all the boats to get off the water."

"I'm sorry you were worried. But we got the warning, and Nicholas came right home," Elizabeth assured them. "I told you he was mature and responsible," she added in a teasing tone.

But instead of smiling as Elizabeth hoped, her mother started crying quietly. Elizabeth rushed to her side. "I'm sorry, Mom," she repeated, giving her mother a big hug. "We really did get back as fast as we could."

"I was so afraid we were going to lose you and Steven, too," Mrs. Wakefield whispered as she held her daughter tightly. "I couldn't bear it."

"Oh, Mom." Tears sprang to Elizabeth's eyes. "We didn't mean to scare you. And we're fine! Please don't be sad."

Alice Wakefield wiped at her eyes and laughed shakily. "Once a mother hen, always a mother hen, I guess," she said, doing her best to sound more cheerful. "No matter how big you kids get, I'm always going to worry about you."

Now Steven embraced his mother. Then the four realized that while they had been standing on the front steps talking and hugging, they'd also been getting soaked to the skin by the rain. "Come inside right this minute!" Mrs. Wakefield ordered her family, her eyes twinkling through the traces of tears. "Mother hen says you'd all better change into some dry clothes on the double! I'll have hot chocolate waiting for you in the kitchen."

Elizabeth raced Steven upstairs. Although he lived in a dorm on campus, Steven still kept a lot of his clothes in his room at home.

In her own room Elizabeth shed her wet clothing quickly, changing into a clean pair of jeans and a royal-blue, long-sleeved cotton shirt. She toweled off her hair and then faced the mirror over her dresser, studying her face as she ran a comb through her damp blond hair. The eyes that stared back at her were uniquely her own, and yet at the same time they were just like Jessica's. By this point in her life Elizabeth was used to the fact that she shared a physical identity with her twin.

Shared—or *had* shared?

"Coming back downstairs, Liz?" Steven asked, sticking his head around her bedroom door.

"Yep. Just a minute." Elizabeth brushed her hair back from her face, then fastened it in the back with one big barrette.

Steven flopped down on Elizabeth's bed to wait for her. His eyes met hers in the mirror. "Are you all right? You look pale."

Her hair taken care of, Elizabeth turned away from the mirror. "I'm just so worried," she explained. "And what Mom and Dad said just now, the way they reacted, really shook me up."

"How do you mean?"

"Mom said they were afraid of losing us, too, remember? That sounds like they've already given up on Jessica. Like they think she really is lost—forever."

Steven fiddled with the bedspread, refusing to meet Elizabeth's eyes. "I think they want to believe she's OK. So do I. But, Liz, the outlook isn't good. We have to face that."

"You can face it if you want," Elizabeth declared, dangerously close to another bout of crying. "I can see as well as anybody that the situation seems bad. But I don't believe Jessica's . . ." Her voice trailed off. She couldn't bring herself to complete the sentence.

"That Jess is dead?" Steven finished the sentence for her.

"She can't be," Elizabeth said passionately. "I'd know. I'd *know*," she repeated with conviction.

Steven nodded in understanding. The whole family recognized that there was a strong bond between the twin sisters. On more than one occasion in the past, when they had been miles away from each other, Elizabeth had *felt* that Jessica was in trouble and vice versa. If one twin experienced pain, the other sensed it.

And Elizabeth didn't feel that Jessica had drowned. Instead, she felt that Jessica was alive and safe, and for the moment she had to believe that there was still hope.

Ten

The fluffy clouds that had dotted the morning sky had multiplied and blocked the sun by the time Jessica and Winston finished their shelter and set off into the woods to collect wood and food.

"I'm glad we built that lean-to first thing," Jessica told Winston, looking apprehensively at the darkening sky. "Or rather, I'm glad you gave me a good kick in the behind and made me help!"

Winston grinned. "I knew if I handled you right, I'd have you eating out of my hand eventually," he joked.

"You'd better watch out or I'm going to kick *your* behind!" Jessica threatened with a pretend scowl. She chased Winston for a few yards and then slowed down to a walk. "Phew, I don't have any energy," she observed. "I'm so hungry I feel weak."

"Me, too." Winston stopped to pick up a piece of dry wood, just the right size for a campfire.

"If I were home in Sweet Valley, I'd probably be on my way to the Dairi Burger with Cara and Lila and Amy right now," Jessica reminisced. "I'd order a burger with everything on it, fries, and a chocolate malt. I can almost taste it!" Just thinking about such delicious, unattainable fare made Jessica's stomach feel twice as hollow.

Winston licked his lips. "I'd probably go home and stuff myself with microwave popcorn. That is, if I didn't stop at Guido's Pizza Palace on the way!"

Jessica shook her head, trying to forget the image of hot, crispy french fries doused with ketchup. "We shouldn't torture ourselves like this," she lectured Winston. "We should be getting ourselves psyched to eat berries and oranges. Just think of how healthy we'll look. It's like one of those low-cholesterol diets."

Winston groaned. "Just what I need."

They each spotted a good piece of firewood at the same moment. Winston insisted on carrying Jessica's log as well as those he'd found. She was glad to hand it over; her mind was occupied with another issue.

"Hey, Winston," she began. "Talking about the Dairi Burger makes me wonder what's going on at home. We've been so busy building the shelter and all, I haven't had any time to think about much else. Do you suppose everybody's really worried about us by now?"

Winston bent over, carefully balancing his armload of firewood, and added another branch to the stack. "Probably," he guessed. "I mean, they've got to be. But they've also got to figure that we'd make it to dry land. There's no such thing as an uncharted isle, no matter what they say. Wherever we are, you can bet it's on the map, and they'll find it."

Jessica hoped that was true, but the island certainly seemed remote and undiscovered to her. She and Winston hadn't come across any signs that people had been there before them.

All along Jessica had been assuming that she would be rescued as a matter of course. But she hadn't thought beyond the rescue itself, to her family and friends waiting at home, not knowing where she was or if she was even alive. She almost liked the idea of being mysteriously lost at sea, with everyone fussing and worrying and talking about her. *People* magazine would probably want her story when she got back to civilization. It was too bad it had to cause her family pain, though.

Jessica suddenly saw a group of orange trees nestled among a grove of small, stubby palms. "Hey, Winston, hold on!" she called. "I'm going to pick some of these."

Taking off her gauze shirt, Jessica used it as a sling, quickly filling it with a dozen of the ripest-looking pieces of fruit. Then she rejoined Winston and displayed her harvest proudly. "So, have I earned my first badge?" she joked.

"Nice going," Winston praised her. Then, shifting the bundle of firewood precariously onto one arm, he held out his left hand. "Here, give me that. I'll carry it."

"It's all right. I can manage," Jessica assured him.

"No, no, I insist." Winston grabbed the makeshift bag from Jessica. "It's the man's job to carry stuff," he said gallantly, "and to protect you frail, delicate women."

Jessica laughed. She was more athletic than

Winston by far, but she wasn't going to argue. She was getting off easy.

Two more peices of firewood later, Winston looked as if he had reached his carrying capacity. But like a true macho man, he wouldn't admit it was too much for him.

"Why don't we head on back?" Jessica suggested, taking pity on Winston. "We've got enough wood and fruit. If we catch a few fish back on the beach, we'll be set for the rest of the day."

"Never say die!" Winston declared, blinking as a drop of sweat rolled into his eye. "I'm game to go a little further. And besides, I think this hill here"—he gestured with his chin toward a narrow, rocky rise to their left—"corresponds to that cliff I saw from the beach when I went for a walk this morning. And from the beach it looked like there were a ton of great-looking fruit bushes on top of the cliff. They might even be blueberries!"

"Blueberries, huh?" Jessica eyed the bluff skeptically. It was steep and dark, and who knew what was at the top? "I don't know, Winston," she said, shaking her head. "Climbing that hill could be more trouble than it's worth. Do you really think we need more fruit?"

Winston seemed to enjoy Jessica's nervous hesitation. It gave him an opportunity to stick his chest out and act brave. "I'll lead the way," he announced. "You'll thank me later when we're eating those blueberries."

Jessica gave in with a sigh. Winston was in the Lewis and Clark explorer mode again, and there was no use arguing with him.

A low rumble of distant thunder met their ears as they started up the hill. Jessica picked her way carefully among the rocks and tree roots, keeping her eyes peeled for lizards and snakes and other disgusting tropical things that might be crawling around, waiting to grab her bare toes.

Even without carrying anything, she found it rough going. Winston, meanwhile, was breathing heavily but doing his best to maintain an air of effortlessness. After ten minutes of steady climbing, they found themselves at the top of the bluff.

"I had no idea we were this high!" Jessica gasped, both thrilled and frightened. Far below them, the gray ocean dashed against the shore, the big waves booming with a hollow, echoing sound. A thin strip of lightning flickered among the rain clouds on the horizon. "I think we'd better pick those blueberries and get out of here," she added, crossing her arms across her chest and shivering in the cool breeze.

"Gotcha." Winston looked around and then made his way along the edge of the cliff. "Just a little further, Jess. I can see the blueberries right over there!"

With a gulp, Jessica followed. She didn't like being so near the edge of the cliff. It was a long way to the beach below.

"Bingo!" Winston exclaimed triumphantly. "What did I tell you? Blueberries galore!"

As soon as the words left his mouth, Winston froze on the cliff in front of her. Jessica, who had picked up her pace in her eagerness to grab some berries and go back down to their shelter, walked right into his back and accidentally bumped her nose on his bony shoulder. "Ouch! Winston, what are you doing?" Jessica asked as she rubbed her nose, annoyed.

In answer, Winston let out a strangled yelp. Jessica looked over his shoulder to find out what had stopped him in his tracks. Had the headhunters found them at last? she wondered, her heart beating wildly.

Something large and dark and furry was blocking the path. Even from a distance Jessica could see its sharp teeth, bared and glinting. The claws on each of its paws looked as long as her fingers, perfect for tearing a person from limb to limb.

"A bear!" Jessica shrieked, her eyes wide with horror. She was as frozen with fear as Winston, her hands clutching his shoulders. "It's a bear," she repeated dumbly, her mouth going dry.

The bear was standing on its back legs by a blueberry bush. Then with an angry growl it dropped to all fours and started shuffling toward them.

Jessica was too frightened to scream, and some instinct told her that the best strategy might be to stay calm and quiet. Although she knew it was a terrible thought, she couldn't help being glad that Winston was positioned between her and the bear.

Jessica had begun to get a grip on herself, but Winston had lost all of his composure. Looking pale and panic-stricken, he whirled around to run away from the bear. "Watch out, Winston!" Jessica whispered fiercely.

Wobbling precariously near the edge of the cliff, Winston dropped everything he had been carrying, including Jessica's shirt that she had used as a sling to carry the fruit.

Still waving his arms wildly, Winston charged

past Jessica and took refuge behind her. Now there was nothing between Jessica and the bear but a few feet—a very few feet—of grassy earth.

Even the day before, capsized in the stormy sea, Jessica hadn't been as frightened. Her life jacket had saved her when she was thrown from the boat, and even though she had lost the jacket, her swimming skill had gotten her to the island. But now she had no weapon, no skills, nothing to save her from the bear's powerful jaws. She couldn't fight a bear the way she had fought the ocean waves!

Jessica stared at the fierce animal, wishing it would disappear, prove a figment of her imagination. Who'd have thought they'd run into a *bear* up there? She had been prepared for boa constrictors, even a cannibal or two, but not a bear!

Then Jessica noticed something. The bear had stopped loping toward them and was now standing on its hind legs again, looking past her. Its big black nose twitched hungrily.

The fruit! Jessica thought. *It's after the fruit, not us!* She turned to look behind her. Sure enough, Winston was cowering next to a bush laden with berries.

Jessica faced the bear again. All of a sudden

she recalled Mr. Russo's lecture on island flora and fauna from the week before. He *had* said something about black bears once indigenous to the coastal region but now extremely rare on the California mainland. Jessica took a closer, calmer look at the bear. It was small, not even as tall as she was. Not exactly a grizzly, she thought. But a bear was still a bear, and this one was hungry. She and Winston had to take action before it decided to have them for dinner instead of berries.

Jessica thought of a solution. "Winston, the bear isn't interested in us, it's just trying to get the fruit next to you. Pick some and throw it over the bear's head! It'll go after the fruit and we can escape!" she frantically explained.

But Winston was still completely petrified. He didn't move or speak in response to Jessica's command. She would have to distract the bear on her own.

Reaching over and grabbing a handful of berries, Jessica lobbed them over the bear's head. The bear sniffed, curious, but didn't turn around. Jessica tossed a second handful. This time some of the berries hit the bear in the nose. The bear let out another low growl, its black eyes glinting.

"Rats!" Jessica muttered desperately. She

ripped an entire branch off the bush and prepared to hurl it. This time she absolutely had to get it right—there was no time left. She wasn't an expert on wild animal behavior, but she knew a bear about to charge when she saw one.

At that instant a deafening crack of thunder split the air around them. As if a switch had been pulled somewhere, the rain started abruptly. It came down in sheets, and Jessica was soaked to the skin in a matter of seconds.

With a frustrated bellow, the bear spun around on its paws and lumbered off into the trees in the opposite direction.

"C'mon, Egbert, let's get out of here!" Jessica shouted. But Winston still didn't move. He was shaking like a leaf, his eyes as wide as saucers.

Jessica grabbed his arm and gave it a tug. Winston stumbled forward, in a daze. Taking Winston's hand and holding it tightly in hers, Jessica led the way in an out-and-out sprint down the hillside.

The rainstorm rattled the palm-leaf walls of the shelter, but inside it had stayed warm and dry so far. Jessica had collapsed on the makeshift sofa on her side of the vine curtain and was now wringing the water out of her dripping hair. Winston, in the meantime, had slunk into his own side without saying a word to Jessica.

Once she had caught her breath and gotten over the shock of encountering the bear, Jessica began to feel hungry again. The rain was still falling steadily; it could last for hours. One thing was for sure, she couldn't get any wetter. She might as well make another trip to the orange grove. A few oranges would tide her over for a while at least, she decided.

"Hey, Winston!" she called. There was no answer. Jessica peered through the vines. She could see Winston, sitting with his back to her and his shoulders slumped forward dejectedly.

"Winston, do you want to walk with me to the orange trees and get a snack?" She tried to make a joke, hoping to lift his spirits. "I hear they're having a rainy-day special—all you can eat for free!"

He still didn't answer. If anything, Winston's shoulders had slumped down even further. It was as if he were trying to sink right into the sand and disappear.

Then it struck Jessica: Winston was probably still scared. He was afraid to go back into the woods and run into another bear!

For a few seconds Jessica fought to stifle a

giggle. *Some he-man!* she thought, recalling how Winston's bravado had vanished in the face of the bear. Then the urge to laugh passed, and Jessica felt guilty. She had been as frightened as Winston, only she'd had the presence of mind to get out of there. And Winston had been so sweet and thoughtful all day. He had shared his food with her that morning, even though she had acted like a snob.

The least I can do is share something with him, she decided.

Jessica got to her feet. "Winston, I'm going out anyway. I don't mind the rain. I'll bring you back some oranges."

"I don't want any," Winston grunted, still not looking in her direction.

"But you've got to be starving," Jessica argued. "Seriously, it's no problem. I can use a palm leaf to carry them and bring back a whole bunch."

"I can't take anything from you," Winston said in a low, mournful voice. He heaved a big sigh. "I don't deserve anything. I dropped all our food and firewood and your shirt. I ran away from the bear. I'm a failure."

"Winston!" Jessica exclaimed. She barged through the vines into his half of the shelter. "Don't be an idiot!"

"Well, it's true, isn't it?" Winston faced Jessica, an embarrassed expression on his face. "I acted like a big coward. I'm a failure," he repeated.

Jessica shook her head vigorously, her wet hair swinging. "I can't believe you!" She sat down on the palm fronds next to Winston and gave his arm a shake. "Just because you made one mistake—and, believe me, I wasn't exactly running up to give that bear a hug myself!—that doesn't mean you're a failure."

"It doesn't?" Winston sounded as if he would like to be convinced.

"No way. You know perfectly well that if it hadn't been for you, I'd be sitting out there in the rain waiting for the rescuers." She flashed Winston a teasing smile. "I might still have the shirt that you dropped over the cliff, but that's about all I'd have! Without you, I wouldn't have known the first thing to do."

"You really mean that?" Winston mumbled.

"Do I ever," Jessica said sincerely. "I'd be hungry, wet, lonely, and scared. You took charge, and we got something done. I really admire that."

Winston sat up a little straighter. He ran a hand through his hair, smoothing it self-consciously. "Yeah?"

"Yeah." Now that Jessica knew Winston was feeling better about himself, she couldn't resist kidding him a little bit. "But, Winston, you should have seen your face up on the hill just now!" She doubled over, unable to suppress her pent-up laughter any longer. "You looked like an extra in *The Night of the Living Dead*!"

Winston didn't laugh along with her. Instead, he looked hurt. Jessica stopped giggling and gently put a hand on Winston's arm. "Sorry, Winston. I didn't mean that. I was just trying to be funny. I guess I should leave that department to you, huh?"

Winston cracked a weak smile. "I guess so."

They sat for a few minutes in silence, listening to the patter of raindrops on the roof. Then Winston cleared his throat. "Um, thanks, Jessica," he said, somewhat shyly. "Thanks for cheering me up."

"Hey, it was nothing." She punched him lightly on the shoulder. "And besides, I meant every word I said. I do admire you."

Winston shook his head with a disbelieving smile. "You know, if anyone had ever told me I'd hear Jessica Wakefield say something like that to me, I'd have thought they were crazy!"

Jessica laughed. "Am I all that bad?" she asked.

"Well . . ." Winston hesitated. "I've got to admit, I always thought you were sort of, well, uh, a little bit of a snob."

Jessica raised one eyebrow and gave Winston a furious look. But she knew she couldn't really get mad at him. It might sting a little, but he was telling the truth. "Well," she said, deciding that if it was time for true confessions, she could at least get a lick in, "*I* always thought *you* were a complete goon!"

Winston chuckled. "You've got me there," he confessed. "I'm guilty as charged. But, you know, it's not always a barrel of laughs being the class clown." Jessica groaned at the joke, but Winston continued. "I mean, it's like any label, I guess. I'm the class clown so I always have to do something funny. I have a reputation to live up to, you know? And sometimes I know I go overboard with it." Winston looked to Jessica for confirmation. "Like yesterday, on the field trip. I was driving you crazy playing pranks on you, wasn't I?"

Jessica nodded. "But now that I think about it, I was mostly annoyed because you kept getting in my way when I was trying to flirt with Ken," she admitted. "If it hadn't been for that, maybe I'd have had a better sense of humor about it!" She twisted a strand of damp hair

125

around her index finger. "Well, I guess we've learned something about each other, huh?"

"You bet." Winston leaned back against the rocks, his hands deep in his pockets. Neither of them spoke, but Jessica knew his thoughts were running along the same lines as hers. She had found out that Winston had a strong side as well as a silly one. Maybe he had panicked at the sight of the bear, but he was still generous, responsible, and forgiving. She could tell that he had come to appreciate her, too. And she had a feeling that when—or was it *if?*—they returned to Sweet Valley High, their relationship would never be quite the same.

Without a word, Winston slipped his arm around Jessica's slender shoulders and gave her a friendly squeeze. Side by side, they settled back on the palm leaves to wait out the storm.

Eleven

The rain stopped just before sunset, not a moment too soon for Jessica. She and Winston had played every game they could think of: twenty questions, truth or dare, charades. Truth or dare had led to an in-depth conversation about the social life at Sweet Valley High, which in turn had led to an onset of major-league moping by Winston, who missed his girlfriend, Maria.

"What if we're never rescued?" Winston moaned. "Maria will find someone else. I always knew she was too good for a geek like me. I always knew it was just a matter of time before some huge, handsome football player came along and stole her right out from under my nose."

"Oh, shut up, Winston." Jessica was feeling less than sympathetic. Her newfound affection for Winston was already eroding as his whining continued. In truth, Jessica was mostly irritated because Winston had started her thinking about her own family and friends. For the first time, she felt depressed.

Jessica and Winston emerged from their shelter to find a calmer ocean and a breathtaking purple, scarlet, and orange sky. After setting up a fishing pole made out of a branch, some string, and a safety pin from the emergency kit, Winston settled down on the beach to construct the world's biggest sand castle. Jessica knew she should make an attempt to rustle up some food as well, but she didn't have the strength. Instead, she wandered lazily along the shore, looking for pretty shells that might have been washed up by the storm.

The island was unbelievably peaceful. The birds had started singing again, and their music was the only sound to be heard beyond the lapping of the waves and the rustling of the palms in the gentle breeze. Jessica sighed. The air smelled rain-fresh, and the island looked like something out of a cruise ship brochure.

So how come I feel like crying? Jessica thought as she sat down on a big piece of driftwood at the far end of the beach. She leaned her elbows on her knees, rested her chin in her hands, and stared out at the sea. She had only been a castaway for roughly twenty-four hours, but it felt like months. Sure, she was getting along fine with Winston. Who'd have thought he would turn out to be such a good traveling companion? And she had missed a day of school and her tan was a shade darker than it had been yesterday.

But they still hadn't been rescued. They hadn't even seen a boat anywhere near the island. And Jessica wasn't looking forward to spending another night there, even though she had a nice dry shelter to sleep in. At the moment what she wanted more than anything else in the world was to curl up in her very own bed at home.

Jessica half shut her eyes, squinting at the sinking sun. What if she was stuck there *forever?* What if, despite what Winston said, the island *was* uncharted and the rescuers never found it? Jessica pictured herself twenty years from now, still dressed in the same ragged bandeau and pair of shorts, with snarled hair down to her feet. How was she supposed to shave her legs and brush her teeth? She imagined growing old with Winston, who would look like Rip Van Winkle after twenty years of solitude, his beard reaching all the way to his knobby knees. "Ugh!" Jessica exclaimed out loud, wrinkling her nose in disgust. What a fate!

She would never see her family again. Elizabeth and Steven would grow up and leave home. Steven would marry Cara, and Elizabeth would marry Jeffrey. And Jessica, simply by virtue of being a castaway, would be deprived of her right to be maid of honor at both ceremonies. Ken Matthews would date some other girl, forgetting Jessica Wakefield ever existed. She would never get to be a senior at Sweet Valley High—she'd miss all the fun of graduation!

All of a sudden Jessica missed her family and friends so much, it hurt. Lila, Cara, Amy . . . At that moment she even would have been glad to see Enid Rollins, her twin's best friend.

"I'll never shop at the Valley Mall again," Jessica wailed to herself. "All the new European fashions will come in at Lisette's, and I won't be there to buy them! I'll be wearing palm leaves while Lila wears the latest Italian leather outfits. It's not *fair!*"

Jessica sniffled, enjoying the new activity of feeling sorry for herself. *I'll never get to dance*

*with Ken Matthews or anyone else at the Beach Disco
again as long as I live. No more greasy fries and
double-chocolate shakes at the Dairi Burger. Some
other girl will take over as co-captain of the cheerlead-
ers and change all the great cheers I made up. I won't
get invited to the next bash Lila throws at Fowler
Crest. Since I'm not there to share it, Liz'll have the
car all to herself and Mom and Dad will probably
give her my bedroom, too. They'll spoil her to death—
they'll probably double her allowance!*

This last was too much for Jessica. A tear of
self-pity squeezed out of one eye and rolled
slowly down her cheek. She had to face the
horrible truth: The best years of her life were
going to be wasted on an island in the middle
of nowhere with Winston Egbert!

Feeling tragic and deprived, Jessica picked a
twig off the sand and ran it through her hair
like a comb. At that moment she felt as if she'd
be willing to do just about anything if it would
guarantee her an immediate airlift off the island. If she was rescued, she was convinced
she would be a changed person. "I'll be nicer if
I get rescued, I promise," she said out loud, as
if taking a vow. "I'll develop the other side of
me that Winston's been talking about." Jessica
figured she had already gotten a head start on
being nicer. She had become friends with Win-

131

ston, after all. She was proud of *that* achievement. It sure wouldn't have happened if they hadn't been shipwrecked together.

She continued bargaining. "I'll make my bed every day and keep my room clean. I'll offer to do the dinner dishes more often, instead of always leaving them for Liz. I'll get a part-time job and start saving up money for college so Mom and Dad won't have to foot the whole bill. I'll—"

Jessica's plans were interrupted by a whirring sound in the distance. She stood up and stared out to sea, straining her eyes. A black dot appeared in the sky and grew larger. It was a helicopter, heading right toward the island!

"Winston, look!" Jessica squealed, springing down the beach and waving her arms. "It's a helicopter! It's the rescuers. We've got to signal them!"

Winston abandoned his sand castle with a triumphant whoop. "Yahoo!" he hollered, jumping up and down. "This way, Mr. Chopper! Come and get us!"

As the helicopter approached the island it dropped ever lower. Jessica and Winston were both screaming at the top of their lungs and doing every sort of attention-getting acrobatic maneuver they could think of. Now they could see the lettering on the side of the helicopter —U.S. Coast Guard—and the pilot could clearly see them. He waved a hand, and Jessica waved back.

Hey, he looks sort of cute, she thought for a second. But she wouldn't have cared if Dr. Frankenstein's monster were flying the helicopter. Only one thing mattered: She was rescued!

Twelve

"Here we are, folks!" the pilot announced as the helicopter touched down on the landing strip at the Coast Guard station. "You're home."

Jessica had borrowed a comb from the cute pilot to work on her hair so she wouldn't be totally hideous when she arrived on the mainland. She wanted to look like a castaway, sure, but a *glamorous* castaway.

Now she was extra glad she had gone to the trouble of fixing her hair. Winston, who was sitting behind her in the helicopter, grabbed her shoulders and gave her a shake. "Jess, look!" he yelped with excitement. "There are about a hundred reporters out there waiting to hear our story!"

Jessica peered through the thick glass window. Sure enough, several men and women carrying news cameras and microphones were gathered on the runway, braving the wind created by the helicopter's propeller in order to be on hand when Jessica and Winston arrived. The pilot had radioed ahead to say he'd found the two missing teenagers.

Jessica felt a thrill of pleasure. She and Winston were *heroes*! Their pictures were going to be plastered on the front page of every newspaper around! They'd probably be the top story on the evening news! Then the invitations to appear on talk shows would roll in. She would be interviewed by Oprah Winfrey, Barbara Walters, maybe even the *60 Minutes* team.

"Maybe we should get lost at sea every week, Winston!" Jessica suggested, winking at him.

Two Coast Guard officers had crossed the runway to meet the newly arrived helicopter. "I'm dropping you off here," the pilot explained. "That pair will protect you from the reporters, and your families should be here any minute now."

Winston gave the pilot a brisk salute. "Thank

you very much for rescuing us, sir," he said formally.

Jessica leaned forward and kissed the pilot on the cheek. "Thanks a million," she echoed, batting her eyelashes admiringly. "They should give you a medal or something. I'll never forget this."

The pilot grinned. "Ditto. So long, kids!"

The helicopter door swung open, and hands reached up to help Jessica and Winston step out. Bending over at the waist, Jessica scurried with the others out of range of the helicopter's propeller. She felt like she was in a movie, or a TV show at least.

The reporters didn't waste a moment. They started calling out questions as soon as Jessica and Winston straightened up. "How did you manage to get to the island without a lifeboat?" "Do you realize Outermost Island is the farthest piece of land from the coast and that beyond it is the open ocean?" "What did you do for food and shelter?" "Did you expect to be rescued?"

Jessica waved a hand imperiously. "One question at a time, please," she requested with the air of someone who gave interviews every day of her life.

"How did you make it to Outermost Island

after your lifeboat capsized?'' asked a tall man whose microphone read WSCN.

The question was addressed to Jessica and Winston both, but Jessica didn't give Winston a chance to open his mouth. "Well, it wasn't easy, let me tell you!" she informed the audience. She tossed her hair dramatically over one tanned shoulder. "First of all, I was *completely* thrown from the lifeboat with no chance to get back in it. Then my life jacket was ripped right off my body not long afterward. The waves were at least twenty feet high!"

There were oohs and ahs of interest and amazement. Jessica had to restrain herself from purring with satisfaction. "What did you do? Were you scared? Did you think you would drown?" one woman called out.

"Not for a minute," Jessica declared. "Although the waves were incredibly treacherous and I knew I was miles from anywhere, I also knew I was a pretty good swimmer. So I just started swimming."

"How long would you estimate it took you to swim to Outermost Island?" the first reporter pressed her.

"Oh, hours." It *had* seemed like hours, Jessica thought, feeling justified in her exaggeration. "I swam every stroke I could think of—crawl, side, breast, you name it. I alternated to preserve my strength. At one point I thought I saw a school of sharks!" That was an outright lie, but it was worth it to hear the reporters gasp. "Fortunately I spotted land just then," Jessica added, relieving their suspense. "I crawled up onto the beach just as the sharks were closing in."

"You were on the island for an entire day and night," a journalist from *The Sweet Valley News* observed. "What were the conditions there? How did you handle your shipwrecked situation?"

"Well, of course I'd never been shipwrecked before," Jessica told the group. "But right away I realized it might be a while before I'd get off the island and that I'd have to gather food and build a shelter."

As Jessica spoke Winston's mouth dropped open with disbelief. Jessica ignored him. "So," she continued, illustrating her story with animated gestures, "because it looked like another storm was on its way, I took care of the shelter first thing. I collected wood and palm fronds and built a lean-to against a pile of rocks. Oh, and I discovered Winston," she added almost as an afterthought. "He'd washed up on the island, too! And he had an emergency kit from the lifeboat with string and matches and a Swiss army knife. That helped a lot," Jessica said in praise of Winston.

Winston pulled his shoulders up and cleared his throat. "Yes, I—"

"*Then* I put my mind to the question of food," Jessica said, interrupting Winston. "It was easy to make a fishing pole with a branch and some string. We caught some fish and cooked them over a campfire. We also gathered berries and oranges." Jessica briefly considered telling them about the bear incident, leaving out the part about Winston's wimpiness, of course—she was too kind to make *that* public. Instead, she would embellish the part where she took control of the situation by throwing the fruit to distract the hungry animal. She'd tell them the bear had attacked their shelter—that was it! And that she had chased it away single-handedly with a flaming branch from the campfire.

Just then Jessica caught Winston's eye. He had one eyebrow raised comically, as if to say, "Now what?" Jessica decided she would save the bear episode for her family and friends. "And that was about all there was to it!" she concluded nonchalantly, as if surviving on a deserted island wasn't much harder than a tropical vacation.

"What about you, Winston?" one of the reporters shouted out. "It sounds as if Jessica really took charge of the survival effort. What did you contribute?"

Now that Winston had his chance in the spotlight, he hesitated. Jessica realized she hadn't left much for him to tell, but if she knew Winston, that wouldn't stop him. Turning her head slightly so that the reporters couldn't see, Jessica gave him a broad wink. Winston grinned. "Who, me?" he asked jovially. "I provided the entertainment! It was an ideal opportunity to practice my stand-up-comedian routine. Jessica couldn't walk out on me—she was stranded!"

The reporters chuckled appreciatively, and Winston smiled, ready to crack a few more deserted-island jokes.

At that instant Jessica saw her family. "Mom! Dad! Liz! Steve!" she shrieked.

The Wakefields had just emerged from the Coast Guard station, and they were hurrying across the blacktop runway. Right behind them were Winston's parents and Maria.

Jessica pushed her way through the crowd of reporters, with Winston at her heels. A moment later she was engulfed in hugs as her parents, Elizabeth, and Steven all tried to put their arms around her at once.

"Jessica, I can't believe we've got you back again!" Tears of joy flowed down Mrs. Wakefield's face. "When they found the empty lifeboat, we thought . . ." She was too choked up to finish the sentence.

"We thought our little girl . . ." Mr. Wakefield's own eyes sparkled with grateful tears.

"I'm OK," Jessica said, her words muffled against her father's chest. "I'm fine—really."

Jessica was conscious of the news cameras rolling as she turned away from her parents to give Elizabeth and Steven a chance to hug her. But she didn't have to put on much of an act. She had never been so happy to see her family in all her life!

A few feet away Winston was enjoying a similar reunion. Mrs. Egbert, usually very reserved and sophisticated, was sobbing happily as she embraced Winston. Meanwhile, Mr. Egbert was holding Winston's right hand, which he kept shaking vigorously. "We're so glad to see you, Winston. We were so worried. We didn't know what we'd ever do without you."

Winston was finally able to wiggle out of his mother's arms. After giving both his parents a kiss, he turned to Maria, who had been standing to one side, looking on. After grabbing Maria by the waist, Winston picked her right up off the ground and swung her around in a circle.

Laughing and crying at the same time, Maria pretended to give Winston a lecture. "What did you think you were doing, scaring everybody like that?"

"What are you talking about?" Winston said innocently. "Jessica and I just hadn't finished our field trip report. We went back to the island to do some more research!"

Maria laughed and swatted him on the shoulder. "Put me down," she told him, giggling. "Please?"

"Nope," Winston refused, his voice cracking with emotion. "I didn't think I'd ever get to hold you again. I'm not letting you go so easily."

The Wakefields walked slowly in the direction of the parking lot on the far side of the Coast Guard station. Everyone was trying to talk at once. Mr. and Mrs. Wakefield, Steven, and Elizabeth wanted to hear all about Jessica's experience on Outermost Island, while Jessica wanted to know what she had missed at home and in school. She felt as if she'd been away from Sweet Valley forever.

"How's Prince Albert?" Jessica asked, eagerly referring to the Wakefields' lovable dog, a somewhat pampered golden retriever. "Did I get any mail? Have Lila and Cara and Amy and my other friends all been totally frantic about me?"

"Fine, no, and of course," Mrs. Wakefield said, responding to her questions in order.

"Forget about all that!" Elizabeth exclaimed impatiently. "Tell us what you've been doing! How did you get to the island? How did Winston get there? What was it like? What did you see? What did you eat?"

"Well." Jessica paused before launching into another description of the ordeal. She wrapped an arm around her twin's waist, giving her a playful squeeze. "Are you sure you want to hear all the gory details, Liz?"

Elizabeth smiled. She had a feeling she was about to be treated to Jessica's version of history —anything *but* "the whole truth and nothing but the truth." "Sure," Elizabeth encouraged Jessica. "Spill it. I haven't heard a good fairy tale in a while!"

"You brat!" Jessica pinched Elizabeth in the side. Elizabeth retaliated by tickling her.

"It looks like everything's back to normal,"

Mr. Wakefield observed, squeezing his wife's hand.

She smiled at her two daughters, who were walking beside her. "You mean everything's back to crazy," she corrected him.

"C'mon, Mom, you love it," Jessica teased, flashing her mother an irresistible smile. "You wouldn't have it any other way."

Thirteen

"Finished!" Elizabeth announced as she dropped the typeset pages for the next edition of *The Oracle* into a box marked "To Printer." "I've just proofread the definitive article on Jessica and Winston's shipwreck," she told Olivia Davidson, who had been working along with her in the cluttered office of Sweet Valley High's newspaper. "I hope that it answers everyone's questions—and that I never have to hear about it again!"

Olivia pushed her frizzy brown hair back from her forehead and smiled sympathetically. "That bad, huh?"

"It's all anyone wants to talk about lately," Elizabeth said. "And Jessica's not doing anything to end the gossip. She's told me seventeen versions of her own story, each one more unbelievable than the last!" Elizabeth sighed deeply and rolled her eyes in mock exasperation. Still, she couldn't help smiling as she thought of how Jessica had managed to turn a calamity into another opportunity to be the center of attention.

"Leave it to your twin," Olivia said, echoing Elizabeth's musings. "She gets marooned with a guy on a desert island, while some of us around here barely remember what it's like to go on a date."

"Oh, Olivia," Elizabeth joked, "I don't think an overnight trip with Winston is exactly a romantic fantasy come true. Would you really have wanted to be in Jess's place?"

Olivia pretended to consider it for a moment, then she laughed. "I guess not," she admitted. She grew more serious. "It's just that I haven't really been interested in anyone since Roger and I split up, and I'm ready for a little excitement."

Olivia stood up and put her own work in the folder for the printer. "I'm about done here, too," she said. "Wait a minute, and I'll walk out with you."

The hallway was quiet as Elizabeth and Olivia left the office. "Gee, I had no idea it was so late," Elizabeth said. "It looks like we're the only ones left in the building."

Just then footsteps sounded from both ends of the corridor.

"Liz! Olivia! I'm so glad I found you!" Penny Ayala, editor in chief of *The Oracle* called from one direction.

"Lizzie! Wait up! I've got exciting news!" Jessica called from the other.

"Looks like you spoke too soon," Olivia commented to Elizabeth.

Penny reached them first. "I wanted to let you two know that we're going to have to rearrange the layout of some pages in the paper tomorrow for an announcement," she said, a little out of breath. "Mr. Collins just told me that Sweet Valley High is going to have an experimental program of minicourses. Local experts will come in to teach classes like acting, filmmaking, photography, even computer-game design. It'll be a chance to study subjects the school doesn't offer or that students can't fit into their schedules."

"So you heard, too," Jessica said, coming up behind them with Lila Fowler at her side. "Sounds great, doesn't it? And the best part of it all is *no grades*."

"I heard Veronica Barry, the artist, was going to give a course in jewelry design," Lila said. "But I also heard there might be a modeling course."

"Ugh!" said Jessica. "Why would you want to take either one of those courses with a hundred other girls? I'm considering electronics. Just think, if I sighed up for that, I'd be surrounded by a roomful of boys for an hour every day."

While Jessica and Lila argued over which minicourse to take, Olivia considered the news. What she had told Elizabeth a few moments earlier was true. Her life was in a real rut lately. She went to classes, worked on the paper, and spent time with her friends, but her heart wasn't in it. It was as though she were waiting for something to happen, even though she didn't know exactly what it was.

Maybe minicourses had something to do with it, and not just because they would mean a chance to take a new class. Sure, that would be fun. Olivia had always wanted to know more about photography, for instance. But minicourses would also mean a major change in her dull routine, a chance to meet new people, especially boys. Everyone in her usual classes was so used to thinking of Olivia and Roger as a couple that Olivia suspected the boys she already knew wouldn't even think of asking her out.

But if she was taking a new course, with new boys who didn't think of her that way. . . . She imagined herself in photography class, developing her pictures in the darkroom. A tall, handsome boy would walk in, someone she didn't know, had never even seen before. Their eyes would meet, and a charge of electricity would pass between them—

"Olivia, did you hear me?" Elizabeth was saying.

"Hmm?" Olivia said dreamily. Jessica, Elizabeth, Lila, and Penny were all staring at her, waiting for her to speak.

"I said minicourses sound terrific, don't they?"

"Oh, yes," Olivia agreed. "Terrific." She felt her cheeks grow warm, as if the others could somehow know what wild thoughts she had been having.

Wild, maybe. But as they all walked together

out of the building, Olivia couldn't shake the feeling that something terrific *was* waiting for her just around the corner.

Will Olivia Davidson find the romance she's dreaming of when minicourses come to Sweet Valley High? Find out in Sweet Valley High #57, **TEACHER CRUSH.**

☐	27416 SLAM BOOK FEVER #48	$2.95
☐	27477 PLAYING FOR KEEPS #49	$2.95
☐	27596 OUT OF REACH #50	$2.95
☐	27650 AGAINST THE ODDS #51	$2.95
☐	27720 WHITE LIES #52	$2.95
☐	27771 SECOND CHANCE #53	$2.95
☐	27856 TWO BOY WEEKEND #54	$2.95
☐	27915 PERFECT SHOT #55	$2.95
☐	27970 SHIPWRECKED! #56	$2.95

Prices and availability subject to change without notice

Buy them at your local bookstore or use this page to order.

MURDER AND MYSTERY STRIKES

SWEET VALLEY HIGH

America's favorite teen series has a hot new line of
Super Thrillers!

It's super excitement, super suspense, and super thrills as Jessica and Elizabeth Wakefield put on their detective caps in the new SWEET VALLEY HIGH SUPER THRILLERS! Follow these two sleuths as they witness a murder . . . find themselves running from the mob . . . and uncover the dark secrets of a mysterious woman. SWEET VALLEY HIGH SUPER THRILLERS are guaranteed to keep you on the edge of your seat!

YOU'LL WANT TO READ THEM ALL!